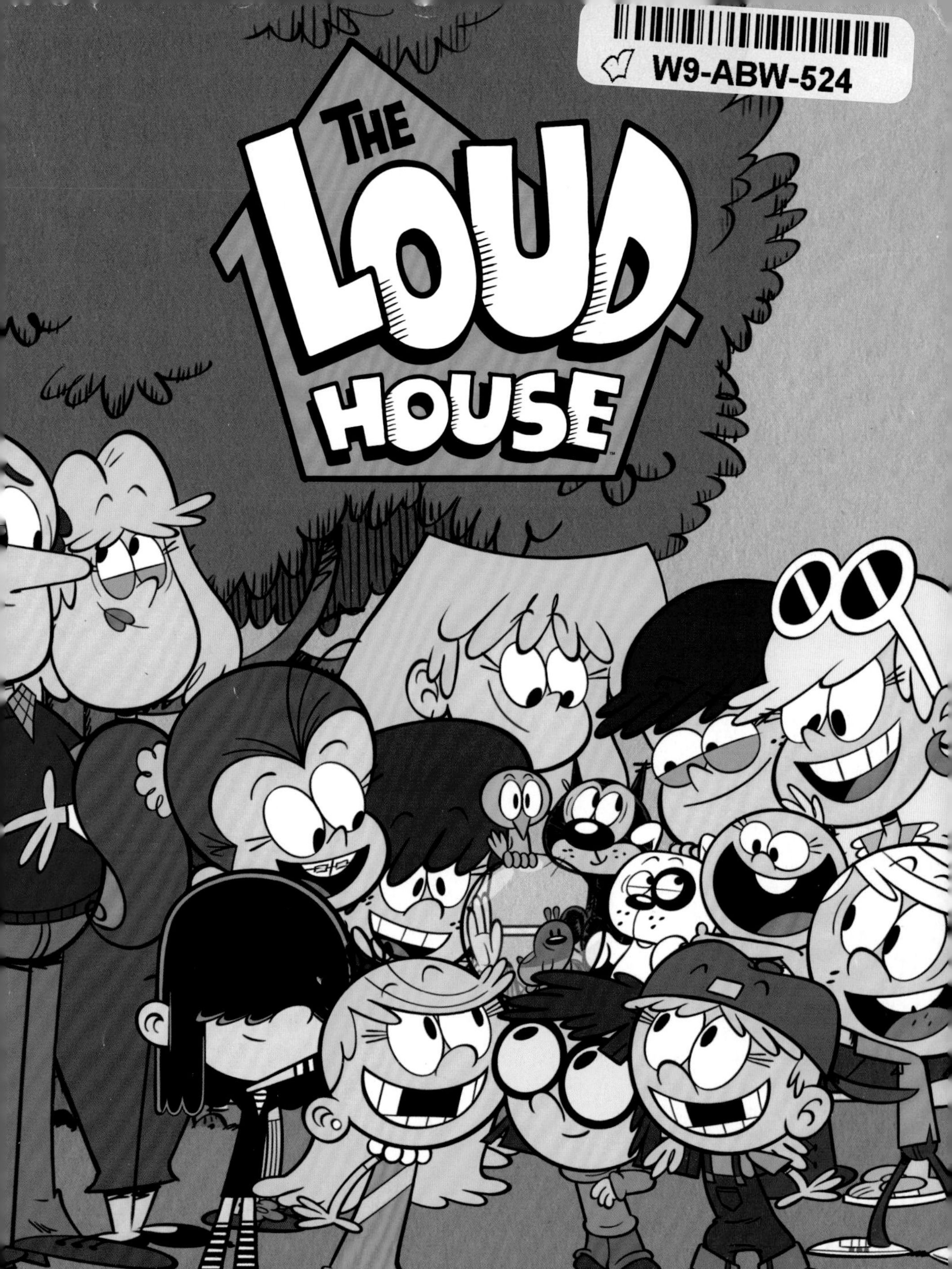
THE LOUD HOUSE

#11 "WHO'S THE LOUDEST?"

PAPERCUTZ
New York

nickelodeon GRAPHIC NOVELS AVAILABLE FROM PAPERCUTZ

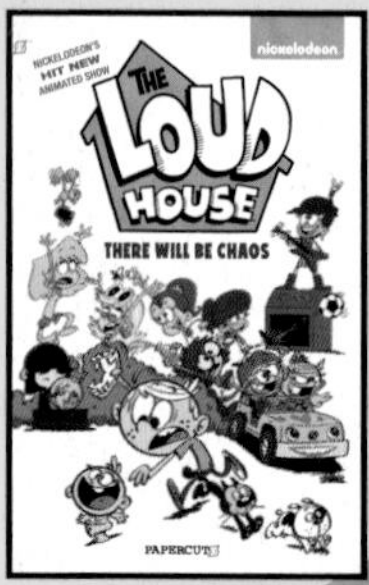

NICKELODEON'S HIT NEW ANIMATED SHOW
THE LOUD HOUSE
THERE WILL BE CHAOS
PAPERCUTZ

THE LOUD HOUSE
#1
"There Will Be Chaos"

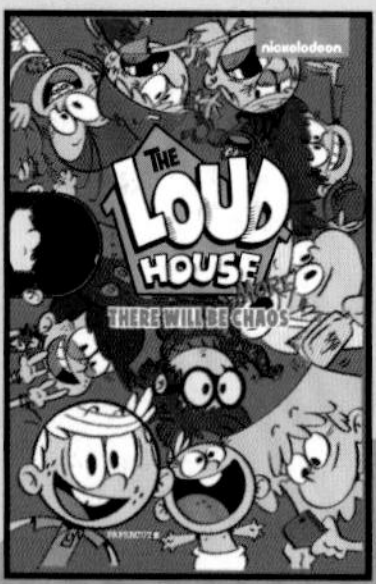

THE LOUD HOUSE
THERE WILL BE CHAOS
PAPERCUTZ

THE LOUD HOUSE
#2
"There Will Be More Chaos"

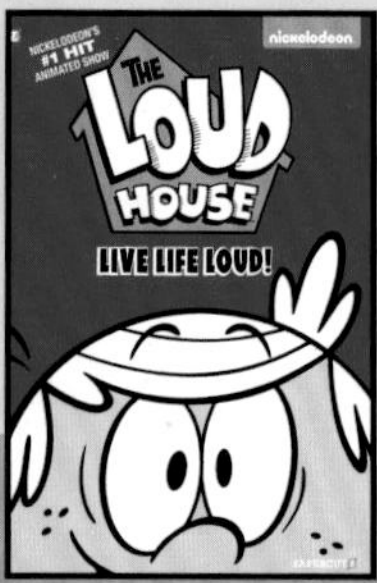

NICKELODEON'S #1 HIT ANIMATED SHOW
THE LOUD HOUSE
LIVE LIFE LOUD!
PAPERCUTZ

THE LOUD HOUSE
#3
"Live Life Loud!"

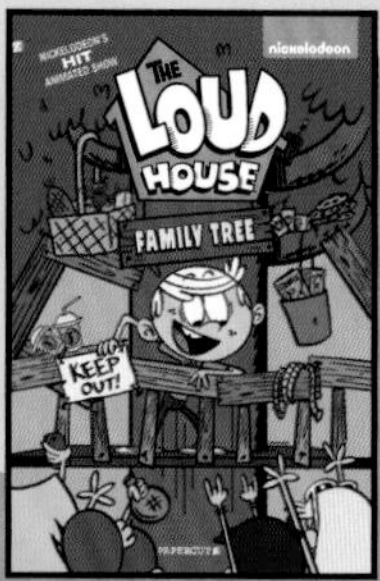

THE LOUD HOUSE
FAMILY TREE
KEEP OUT!
PAPERCUTZ

THE LOUD HOUSE
#4
"Family Tree"

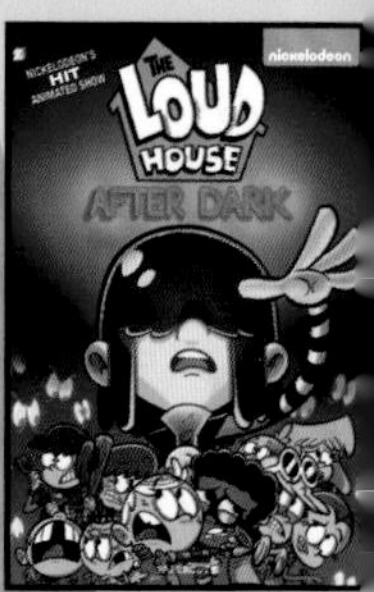

THE LOUD HOUSE
AFTER DARK

THE LOUD HOUSE
#5
"After Dark"

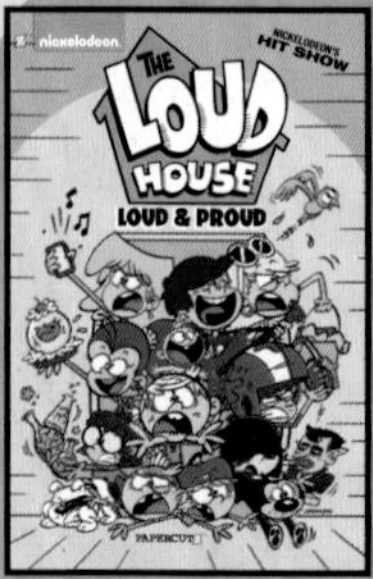

NICKELODEON'S HIT SHOW
THE LOUD HOUSE
LOUD & PROUD
PAPERCUTZ

THE LOUD HOUSE
#6
"Loud and Proud"

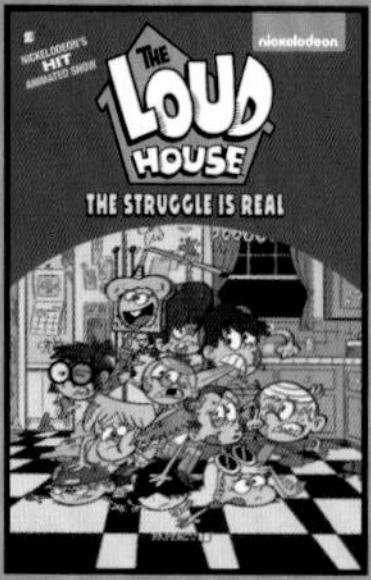

THE LOUD HOUSE
THE STRUGGLE IS REAL

THE LOUD HOUSE
#7
"The Struggle is Real"

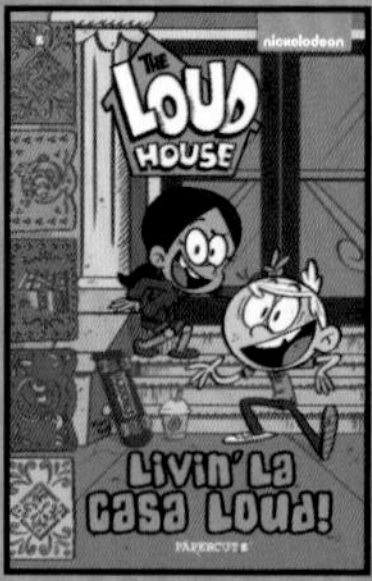

THE LOUD HOUSE
LIVIN' LA CASA LOUD!
PAPERCUTZ

THE LOUD HOUSE
#8
"Livin' La Casa Loud"

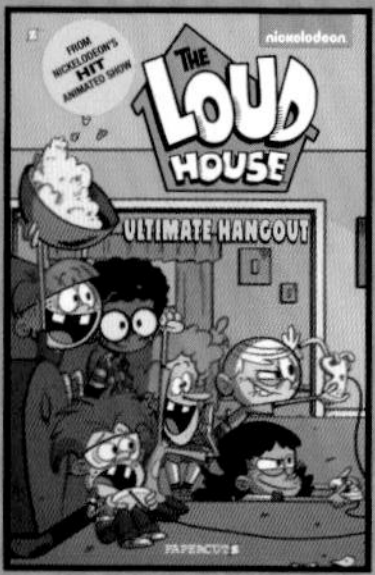

THE LOUD HOUSE
ULTIMATE HANGOUT
PAPERCUTZ

THE LOUD HOUSE
#9
"Ultimate Hangout"

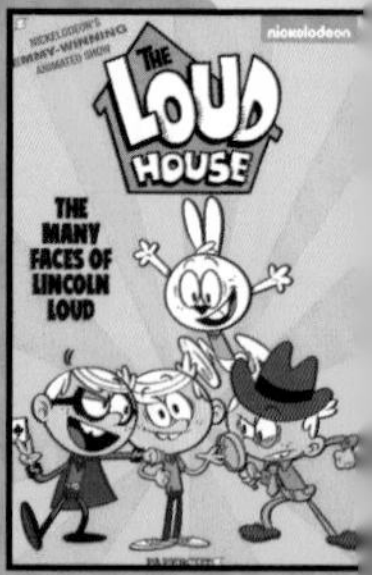

THE LOUD HOUSE
THE MANY FACES OF LINCOLN LOUD

THE LOUD HOUSE
#10
"The Many Faces of Lincoln Loud"

COMING SOON

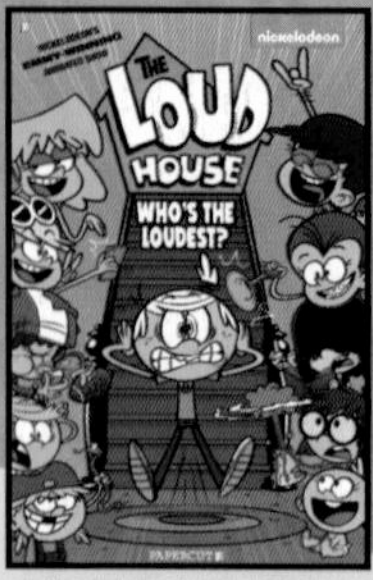

THE LOUD HOUSE
WHO'S THE LOUDEST?

THE LOUD HOUSE
#11
"Who's the Loudest?"

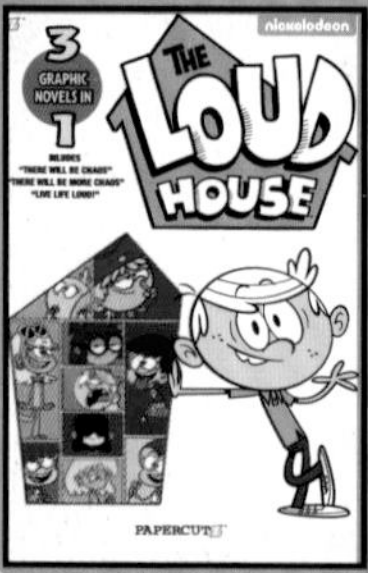

3 GRAPHIC NOVELS IN 1
THE LOUD HOUSE
PAPERCUTZ

THE LOUD HOUSE
3 IN 1
#1

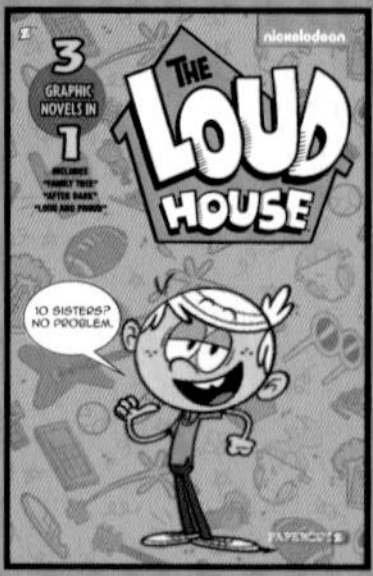

3 GRAPHIC NOVELS IN 1
THE LOUD HOUSE
10 SISTERS? NO PROBLEM.

THE LOUD HOUSE
3 IN 1
#2

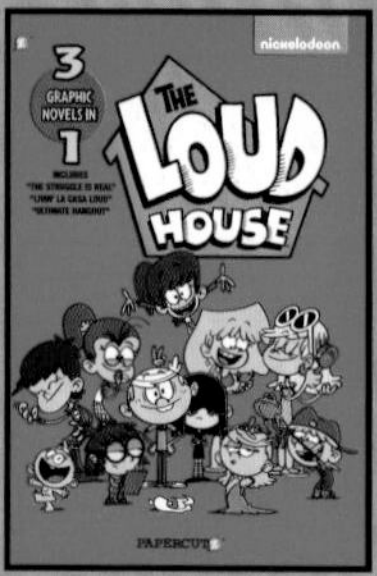

3 GRAPHIC NOVELS IN 1
THE LOUD HOUSE
PAPERCUTZ

THE LOUD HOUSE
3 IN 1
#3

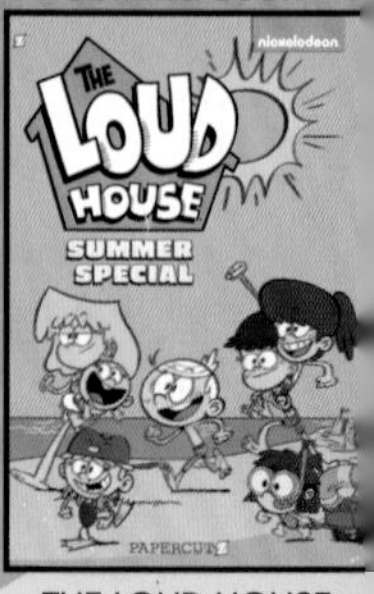

THE LOUD HOUSE
SUMMER SPECIAL
PAPERCUTZ

THE LOUD HOUSE
SUMMER SPECIAL

The Loud House graphic novels and specials are available for $7.99 each in paperback, $12.99 each in hardcover. THE LOUD HOUSE 3 IN 1 graphic novels are available for $14.99 each in paperback only. Available from booksellers everywhere. You can also order online from Papercutz.com, or call 1-800-886-1223, Monday through Friday, 9-5 EST. MC, Visa, and AmEx accepted. To order by mail, please add $5.00 for postage and handling for the first book ordered, $1.00 for each additional book and make check payable to NBM Publishing. Send to: Papercutz, 160 Broadway, Suite 700, East Wing, New York, NY 10038.

books are sold.

THE LOUD HOUSE

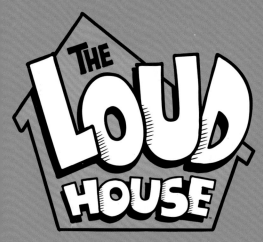

#11 "WHO'S THE LOUDEST?"

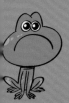

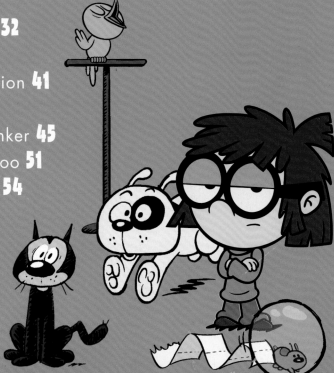

#11 "WHO'S THE LOUDEST?"

"I KNOW WHERE YOU SHOPPED LAST SUMMER"
Caitlin Fein — Writer
Ron Bradley — Artist, Colorist
Wilson Ramos Jr. — Letterer

"HOME SICKNESS"
Kiernan Sjursen-Lien — Writer
Jose Hernandez — Artist, Colorist
Wilson Ramos Jr. — Letterer

"MUSICAL MYRTLE"
Jair Holguin, George Holguin — Writers
George Holguin — Artist, Colorist
Wilson Ramos Jr. — Letterer

"OCEAN 11"
Derek Fridolfs — Writer
Tyler Koberstein — Artist, Colorist
Wilson Ramos Jr. — Letterer

"FREE TO BE ME"
Kiernan Sjursen-Lien — Writer
Zazo Aguiar — Artist, Colorist
Wilson Ramos Jr. — Letterer

"SNACK ATTACK"
Kiernan Sjursen-Lien — Writer
Daniela Rodriguez — Artist, Colorist
Wilson Ramos Jr. — Letterer

"THAT'S A WRAP"
Ron Bradley — Writer, Artist, Colorist
Wilson Ramos Jr. — Letterer

Gabrielle Dolbey
and
Zazo Aguiar — Cover Artists

"MACABRE MUNCHIES"
Kiernan Sjursen-Lien — Writer
Tyler Koberstein — Artist, Colorist
Wilson Ramos Jr. — Letterer

"CANNONBALL RUN"
Jair Holguin, George Holguin — Writers
George Holguin — Artist
Ronda Pattison— Colorist
Wilson Ramos Jr. — Letterer

"CUSTOMER APPRECIATION"
Kiernan Sjursen-Lien — Writer
Jose Hernandez — Artist, Colorist
Wilson Ramos Jr. — Letterer

"ROBOT RUMPUS"
Kiernan Sjursen-Lien — Writer
Melissa Kleynowski — Artist
Princess Bizares— Colorist
Wilson Ramos Jr. — Letterer

"HOOK, LINE, AND STINKER"
Jared Morgan — Writer, Artist, Colorist, Letterer

"ONE, TWO, SWITCHEROO"
Kiernan Sjursen-Lien — Writer
Max Alley — Artist
Peter Bertucci —Colorist
Wilson Ramos Jr. — Letterer

"WHO'S THE LOUDEST?"
Caitlin Fein — Writer
Tyler Koberstein — Artist, Colorist
Wilson Ramos Jr. — Letterer

"OPERATION X-MAS"
Jair Holguin — Writer
George Holguin — Artist, Colorist
Wilson Ramos Jr. — Letterer

JORDAN ROSATO — Endpapers
JAMES SALERNO — Sr. Art Director/Nickelodeon
JAYJAY JACKSON — Design
KEVIN SULLIVAN, ASHLEY KLIMENT, DANA CLUVERIUS, MOLLIE FREILICH, SONIA CANO — Special Thanks
JEFF WHITMAN — Editor
JOAN HILTY — Editor/Nickelodeon
JIM SALICRUP
Editor-in-Chief

ISBN: 978-1-5458-0558-9 paperback edition
ISBN: 978-1-5458-0559-6 hardcover edition

www.papercutz.com

Papercutz books may be purchased for business or promotional use. For information on bulk purchases please contact Macmillan Corporate and Premium Sales Department at (800) 221-7945 x5442.

Printed in Turkey
November 2020

Distributed by Macmillan
First Printing

MEET THE LOUD FAMILY *and friends!*

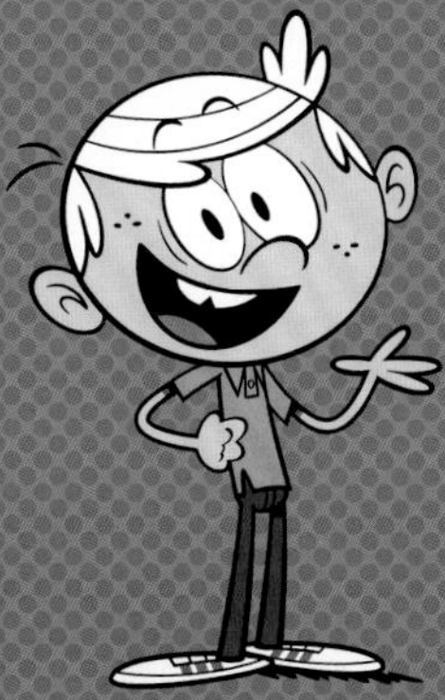

LINCOLN LOUD
THE MIDDLE CHILD (11)

At 11 years old, Lincoln is the middle child, with five older sisters and five younger sisters. He has learned that surviving the Loud household means staying a step ahead. He's the man with a plan, always coming up with a way to get what he wants or deal with a problem, even if things inevitably go wrong. Being the only boy comes with some perks. Lincoln gets his own room – even if it's just a converted linen closet. On the other hand, being the only boy also means he sometimes gets a little too much attention from his sisters. They mother him, tease him, and use him as the occasional lab rat or fashion show participant. Lincoln's sisters may drive him crazy, but he loves them and is always willing to help out if they need him.

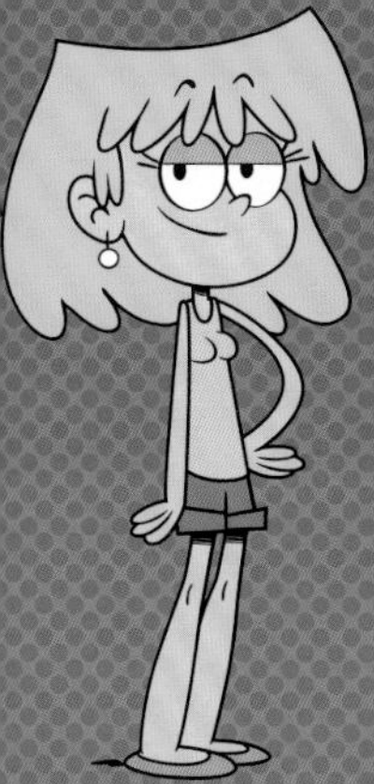

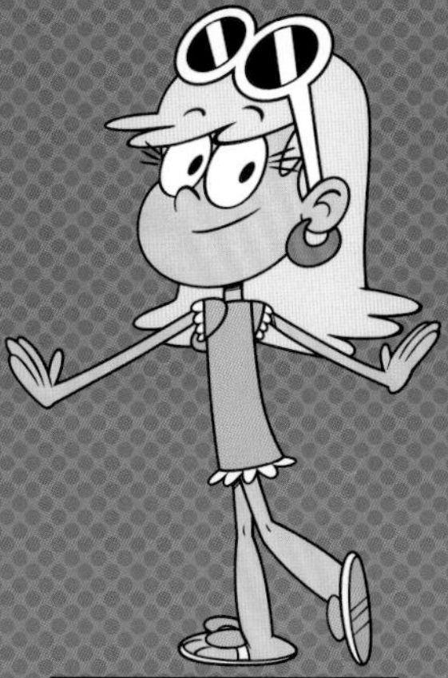

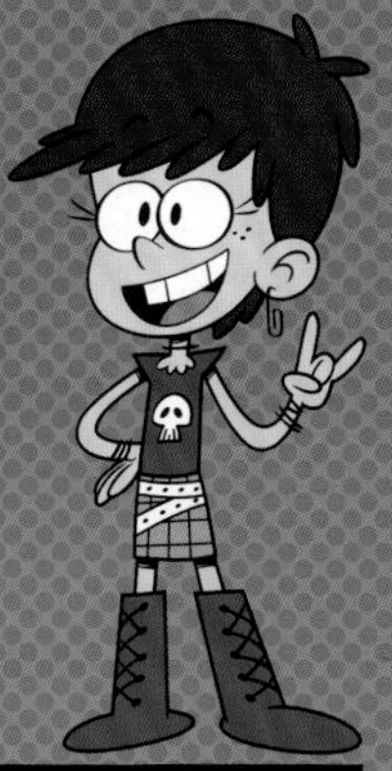

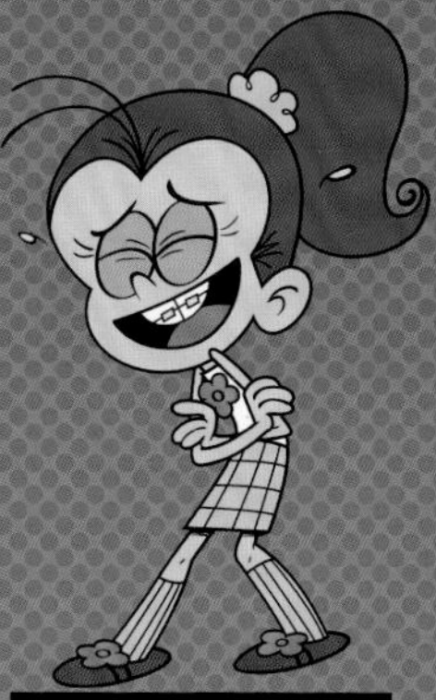

LORI LOUD
THE OLDEST (17)

As the first-born child of the Loud Clan, Lori sees herself as the boss of all her siblings. She feels she's paved the way for them and deserves extra respect. Her signature traits are rolling her eyes, texting her boyfriend, Bobby, and literally saying "literally" all the time. Because she's the oldest and most experienced sibling, Lori can be a great ally, so it pays to stay on her good side, especially since she can drive.

LENI LOUD
THE FASHIONISTA (16)

Leni spends most of her time designing outfits and accessorizing. She always falls for Luan's pranks, and sometimes walks into walls when she's talking (she's not great at doing two things at once). Leni might be flighty, but she's the sweetest of the Loud siblings and truly has a heart of gold (even though she's pretty sure it's a heart of blood).

LUNA LOUD
THE ROCK STAR (15)

Luna is loud, boisterous and freewheeling, and her energy is always cranked to 11. She thinks about music so much that she even talks in song lyrics. On the off-chance she doesn't have her guitar with her, everything can and will be turned into a musical instrument. You can always count on Luna to help out, and she'll do most anything you ask, as long as you're okay with her supplying a rocking guitar accompaniment.

LUAN LOUD
THE JOKESTER (14)

Luan's a standup comedienne who provides a nonstop barrage of silly puns. She's big on prop comedy too – squirting flowers and whoopee cushions – so you have to be on your toes whenever she's around. She loves to pull pranks and is a really good ventriloquist – she is often found doing bits with her dummy, Mr. Coconuts. Luan never lets anything get her down; to her, laughter IS the best medicine.

LYNN LOUD
THE ATHLETE (13)

Lynn is athletic and full of energy and is always looking for a teammate. With her, it's all sports all the time. She'll turn anything into a sport. Putting away eggs? Jump shot! Score! Cleaning up the eggs? Slap shot! Score! Lynn is very competitive, but despite her competitive nature, she always tries to just have a good time.

LUCY LOUD
THE EMO (8)

You can always count on Lucy to give the morbid point of view in any given situation. She is obsessed with all things spooky and dark – funerals, vampires, séances, and the like. She wears mostly black and writes moody poetry. She's usually quiet and keeps to herself. Lucy has a way of mysteriously appearing out of nowhere, and try as they might, her siblings never get used to this.

LOLA LOUD
THE BEAUTY QUEEN (6)

Lola could not be more different from her twin sister, Lana. She's a pageant powerhouse whose interests include glitter, photo shoots, and her own beautiful, beautiful face. But don't let her cute, gap-toothed smile fool you; underneath all the sugar and spice lurks a Machiavellian mastermind. Whatever Lola wants, Lola gets – or else. She's the eyes and ears of the household and never resists an opportunity to tattle on troublemakers. But if you stay on Lola's good side, you've got yourself a fierce ally – and a lifetime supply of free makeovers.

LANA LOUD
THE TOMBOY (6)

Lana is the rough-and-tumble sparkplug counterpart to her twin sister, Lola. She's all about reptiles, mud pies, and muffler repair. She's the resident Ms. Fix-it and is always ready to lend a hand – the dirtier the job, the better. Need your toilet unclogged? Snake fed? Back-zit popped? Lana's your gal. All she asks in return is a little A-B-C gum, or a handful of kibble (she often sneaks it from the dog bowl).

LISA LOUD
THE GENIUS (4)

Lisa is smarter than the rest of her siblings combined. She'll most likely be a rocket scientist, or a brain surgeon, or an evil genius who takes over the world. Lisa spends most of her time working in her lab (the family has gotten used to the explosions), and says her research leaves little time for frivolous human pursuits like "playing" or "getting haircuts." That said, she's always there to help with a homework question, or to explain why the sky is blue, or to point out the structural flaws in someone's pillow fort. Lisa says it's the least she can do for her favorite test subjects, er, siblings.

LILY LOUD
THE BABY (15 MONTHS)

Lily is a giggly, drooly, diaper-ditching free spirit, affectionately known as "the poop machine." You can't keep a nappy on this kid – she's like a teething Houdini. But even when Lily's running wild, dropping rancid diaper bombs, or drooling all over the remote, she always brings a smile to everyone's face (and a clothespin to their nose). Lily is everyone's favorite little buddy, and the whole family loves her unconditionally.

RITA LOUD

Mother to the eleven Loud kids, Mom (Rita Loud) wears many different hats. She's a chauffeur, homework-checker and barf-cleaner-upper all rolled into one. She's always there for her kids and ready to jump into action during a crisis, whether it's a fight between the twins or Leni's missing shoe. When she's not chasing the kids around or at her day job as a dental hygienist for Dr. Feinstein, Mom pursues her passion: writing. She also loves taking on house projects and is very handy with tools (guess that's where Lana gets it from). Between writing, working and being a mom, her days are always hectic but she wouldn't have it any other way.

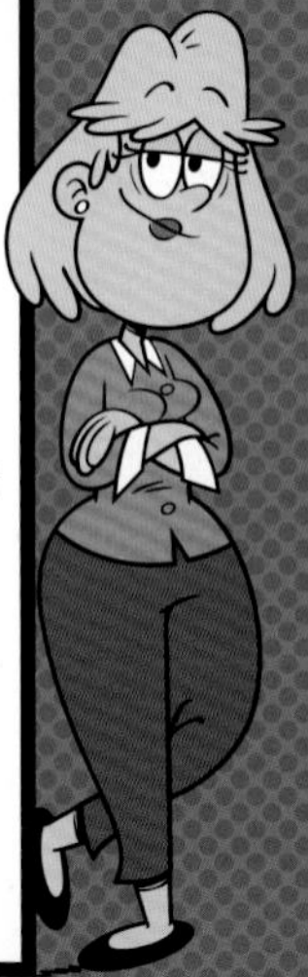

LYNN LOUD SR.

Dad (Lynn Loud Sr.) is a fun-loving, upbeat aspiring chef. A kid-at-heart, he's not above taking part in the kids' zany schemes. In addition to cooking, Dad loves his van, playing the cowbell and making puns. Before meeting Mom, Dad spent a semester in England and has been obsessed with British culture ever since – and sometimes "accidentally" slips into a British accent. When Dad's not wrangling the kids, he's pursuing his dream of opening his own restaurant where he hopes to make his "Lynn-sagnas" world-famous.

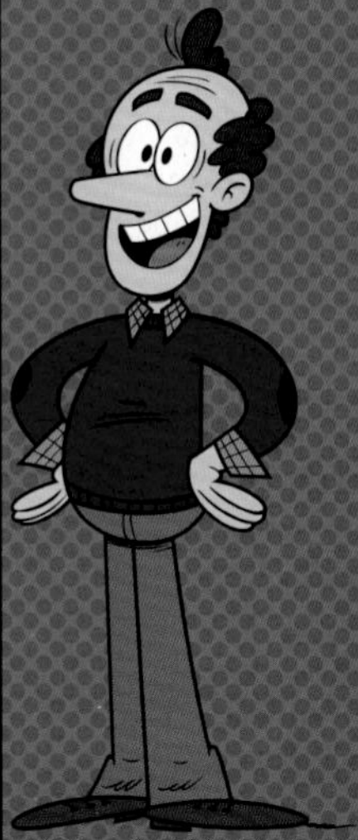

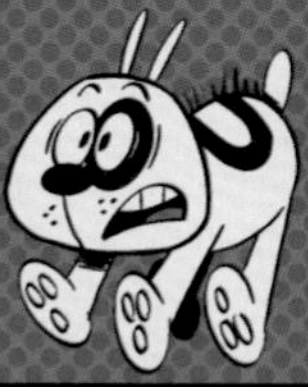

CHARLES

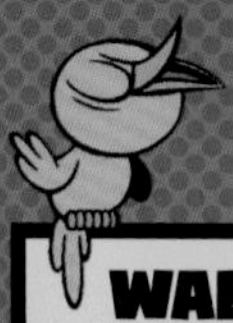

WALT

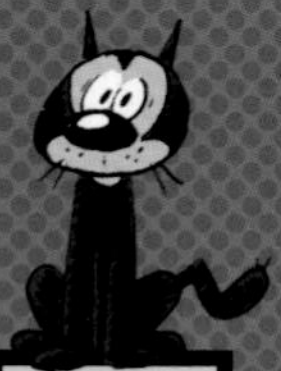

CLIFF

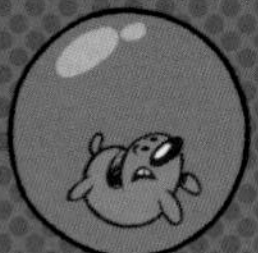

GEO

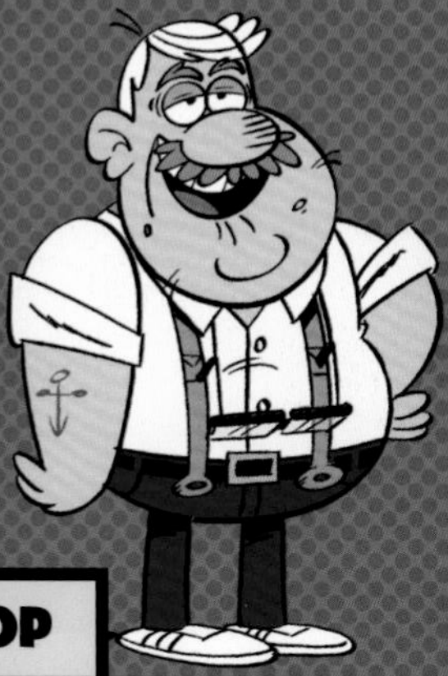

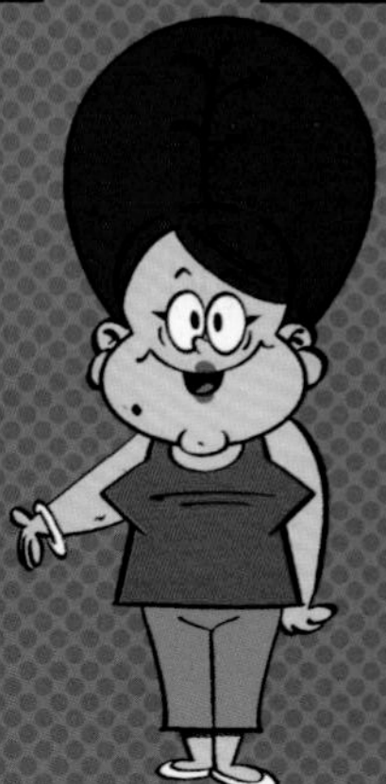

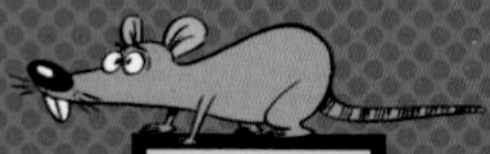

BITEY

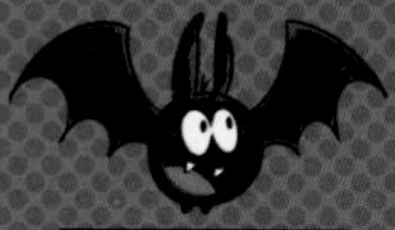

FANGS

POP POP

Albert, the Loud kids' grandfather, currently lives at Sunset Canyon Retirement Community after dedicating his life to working in the military. Pop Pop spends his days dominating at shuffleboard, eating pudding and going on adventures with his pals Bernie, Scoots, and Seymour and his girlfriend, Myrtle. Pop Pop is upbeat, fun-loving and cherishes spending time with his grandchildren.

MYRTLE

Myrtle, or Gran-Gran, is Albert's (Pop Pop's) girlfriend. She loves traveling and hanging out with Albert and the Loud kids. Since she doesn't have grandkids of her own, she's the Loud kids' honorary grandma and can't help but smother them with love.

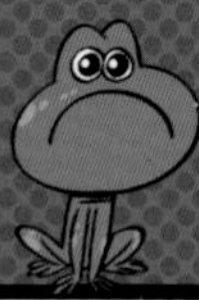

HOPS

CLYDE McBRIDE
THE BEST FRIEND

Clyde is Lincoln's partner in crime. He's always willing to go along with Lincoln's crazy schemes (even if he sees the flaws in them up-front). Lincoln and Clyde are two peas in a pod and share pretty much all of the same tastes in movies, comics, TV shows, toys—you name it. As an only child, Clyde envies Lincoln—how cool would it be to always have siblings around to talk to? But since Clyde spends so much time at the Loud household, he's almost an honorary sibling anyway.

ZACH GURDLE

Zach is a self-admitted nerd who's obsessed with aliens and conspiracy theories. He lives between a freeway and a circus, so the chaos of the Loud House doesn't faze him. He and Rusty occasionally butt heads, but deep down, it's all love.

RUSTY SPOKES

Rusty is a self-proclaimed ladies' man who's always the first to dish out girl advice—even though he's never been on an actual date. His dad owns a suit rental service, so occasionally Rusty can hook the gang up with some dapper duds—just as long as no one gets anything dirty.

LIAM

Liam is an enthusiastic, sweet-natured farm boy full of down-home wisdom. He loves hanging out with his Mee Maw, wrestling his prize pig Virginia, and sharing his farm-to-table produce with the rest of the gang.

STELLA

Stella, 11, is a quirky, carefree girl who's new to Royal Woods. She has tons of interests, like trying on wigs, playing laser tag, eating curly fries, and hanging with her friends. But what she loves the most is tech — she always wants to dismantle electronics and put them back together again.

BENNY STEIN

Benny is Luan's classmate, costar, and boyfriend. He's shy and quirky, but also sweet and earnest. He's not a zany comedian like Luan, but he sure enjoys her sense of humor and appreciates her wicked skills when it comes to prop comedy. Luan keeps Benny laughing, and Benny keeps Luan from sweating the small stuff. And as his marionette, Mrs. Appleblossom, would remind him (in her sassy British accent), it's all small stuff.

RONNIE ANNE SANTIAGO

Ronnie Anne's an independent spirit who's into skating, gaming and pranking. Strong-willed and a little gruff, she isn't into excessive displays of emotion. But don't be fooled – she has a sweet side, too, fostered by years of taking care of her mother and brother. And though her new extended family can be a little overwhelming, she appreciates how loving, caring, and fun they can be.

BOBBY SANTIAGO

Ronnie Anne's older brother, Bobby is a sweet, responsible, loyal high-school senior who works in the family's bodega. Bobby is very devoted to his family. He's Grandpa's right hand man and can't wait to one day take over the bodega for him. Bobby's a big kid and a bit of a klutz, which sometimes gets him into pickles, like locking himself in the freezer case. But he makes up for any work mishaps with his great customer skills – everyone in the neighborhood loves him.

MARIA CASAGRANDE SANTIAGO

She's the mother of Bobby and Ronnie Anne. A hardworking nurse, she doesn't get to spend a lot of time with her kids, but when she does she treasures it. Maria is calm and rational but often worries about whether she's doing enough for her kids. Maria, Bobby, and Ronnie Anne are a close-knit trio who were used to having only each other – until they moved in with their extended family.

HECTOR CASAGRANDE

He's the father of Carlos and Maria and the grandfather of six. The patriarch of the Casagrande Family, Hector wears the pants in the family (or at least thinks he does). He is the owner of the bodega on the ground floor of their apartment building and takes great pride in his work, his family, and being the unofficial "mayor" of the block. He's charismatic, friendly, and also a huge gossip (although he tries to deny it).

ROSA CASAGRANDE

She's the mother of Carlos and Maria and wife to Hector. Rosa is a gifted cook and has a sixth sense about knowing when anyone in her house is hungry. The wisest of the bunch, Rosa is really the head of the household but lets Hector think he is. She's spiritual and often tries to fix problems or illnesses with home remedies or potions. She's protective of all her family and at times can be a bit smothering.

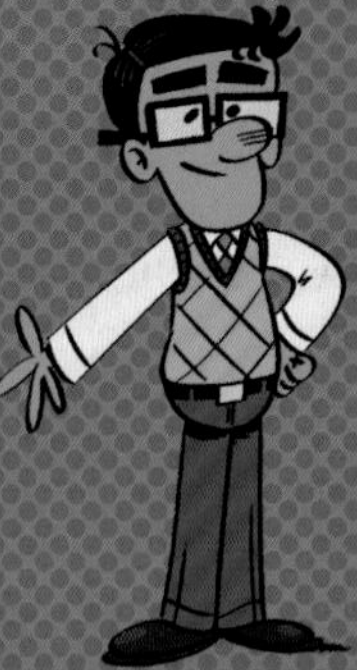

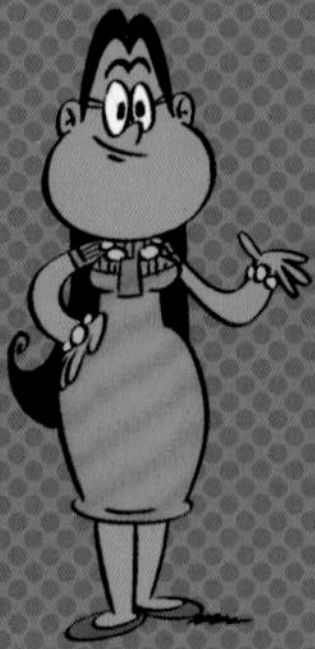

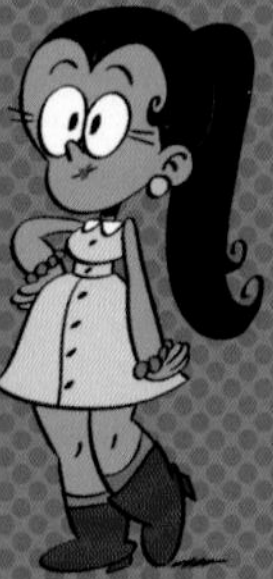

CARLOS CASAGRANDE

He's the father of four kids (Carlota, CJ, Carl, and Carlitos), husband of Frida, and brother of Maria. He's a professor of marine biology at a local college and always has his head in a book. He's a pretty easygoing guy compared to his sometimes overly emotional relatives. Carlos is pragmatic, a caring father, and loves to rattle off useless tidbits of information.

FRIDA PUGA CASAGRANDE

She's the mother to Carlota, CJ, Carl, and Carlitos and wife to Carlos. She's an artist-type, always taking photos of the family. She tends to cry when she's overcome with sadness, anger, happiness... basically, she cries a lot. She's excitable, game for fun, passionate, and loves her family more than anything. All she ever wants is for her entire family to be in the same room. But when that happens, all she can do is cry and take photos.

CARLOTA CASAGRANDE

The oldest child of Carlos and Frida. She's social, fun-loving, and desperately wants to be the big sister to Ronnie Anne. Carlota has a very distinctive vintage style, which she tries to share with Ronnie Anne, who couldn't be less interested.

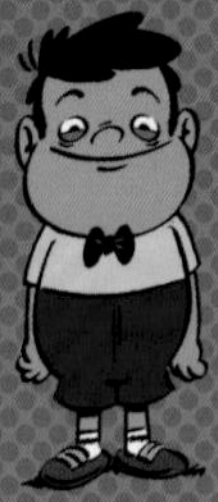

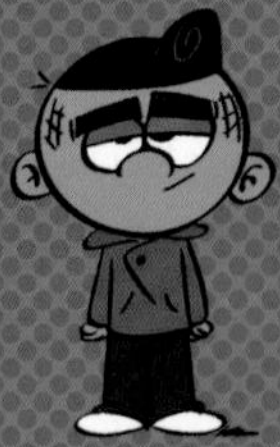

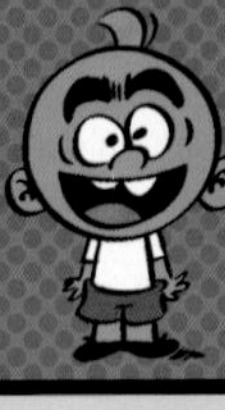

CJ (CARLOS JR.) CASAGRANDE

CJ was born with Down syndrome. He's the sunshine in everyone's life and always wants to play. He will often lighten the mood of a tense situation with his honest remarks. He adores Bobby and always wants to be around him (which is A-OK with Bobby, who sees CJ as a little brother). CJ asks to wear a bowtie every day no matter the occasion and is hardly ever without a smile on his face. He's definitely a glass-half-full kind of guy.

CARL CASAGRANDE

Carlino is 6 going on 30. He thinks of himself as a suave, romantic ladies' man. He's confident and outgoing. When he sees something he likes, he goes for it (even if it's Bobby's girlfriend, Lori). He cares about his appearance even more than Carlota and often uses her hair products (much to her chagrin). He hates to be reminded that he's only six and is emasculated whenever someone notices him snuggling his blankie or sucking his thumb. Carl is convinced that Bobby is his biggest rival and is always trying to beat Bobby (which Bobby is unaware of).

CARLITOS CASAGRANDE

The redheaded toddler who is always mimicking everyone's behavior, even the dog's. He's playful, rambunctious, and loves to play with the family pets.

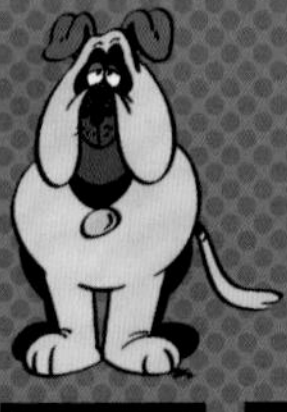

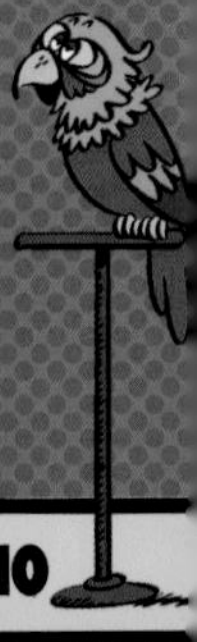

LALO

SERGIO

SAM SHARP

Sam, 15, is Luna's classmate and good friend, who Luna has a crush on. Sam is all about the music – she loves to play guitar and write and compose music. Her favorite genre is rock and roll but she appreciates all good tunes. Unlike Luna, Sam only has one brother, Simon, but she thinks even one sibling provides enough chaos for her.

SULLY

MAZZY

FLIP

The owner of Flip's Food & Fuel, the local convenience store. Flip has questionable business practices – he's been known to sell expired milk and stick his feet in the nacho cheese! When he's not selling Flippees, Flip loves fishing and also sponsors Lynn's rec basketball team.

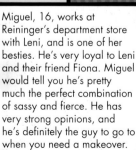

MIGUEL

Miguel, 16, works at Reininger's department store with Leni, and is one of her besties. He's very loyal to Leni and their friend Fiona. Miguel would tell you he's pretty much the perfect combination of sassy and fierce. He has very strong opinions, and he's definitely the guy to go to when you need a makeover.

FIONA

Fiona, 16. Like Miguel, Fiona works at Reininger's department store and is also one of Leni's best friends. Fiona is strong and snarky; her sense of humor is much dryer than the others'. She has little patience for people wasting her time – when it comes to Fiona, you need to get right to the point.

HAIKU

Haiku is Lucy's closest friend and co-president of the Morticians Club. Like Lucy, she keeps a poetry journal, contemplates the meaninglessness of existence, and pines for Edwin, the lead in "Vampires of Melancholia." Haiku's likes include despair and the color black, and her dislikes include cats, sunlight, and people who smile too much.

PERSEPHONE

Persephone is the more fashionable member of the Morticians Club. She's never seen without her parasol, even if it means getting wedged in a bathroom stall because it opened while she was inside. Persephone's favorite food is funeral potatoes, and she'll happily make them even if there's no service being planned.

BORIS

Boris is not only the tallest and baldest member of the Morticians Club, he's also the most playful. Just because he finds life empty and devoid of reason doesn't mean he isn't going to do his best to enjoy it. He's always up for trying something new. Fun fact: Boris isn't his real name – it's Robert. But only his mother calls him that.

DANTE

Dante is another member of the Morticians Club. Unlike Boris he takes things very seriously. Too bad his clumsiness always seems to undermine the dramatic mood he's going for. Dante's very attached to his pet snake, which he keeps in a jar and which no one has ever seen move. It might not be alive – no one is certain.

MORPHEUS

Morpheus is the snarkiest member of the Morticians Club – he believes that being somber and gloomy doesn't mean you can't also be ready with a saucy quip. Morpheus' best friend is his crow, Thorn, and his favorite item of clothing is his vampire cape.

BERTRAND

Bertrand is the former president of the Morticians Club. Unfortunately, he had to resign when his father got a job as a lifeguard on a cruise ship. The club checks in with Bertrand occasionally, but for now he's stuck living a goth's worst nightmare: spending his days in endless sunshine with happy, bubbly people enjoying life to the fullest.

"I KNOW WHERE YOU SHOPPED LAST SUMMER"

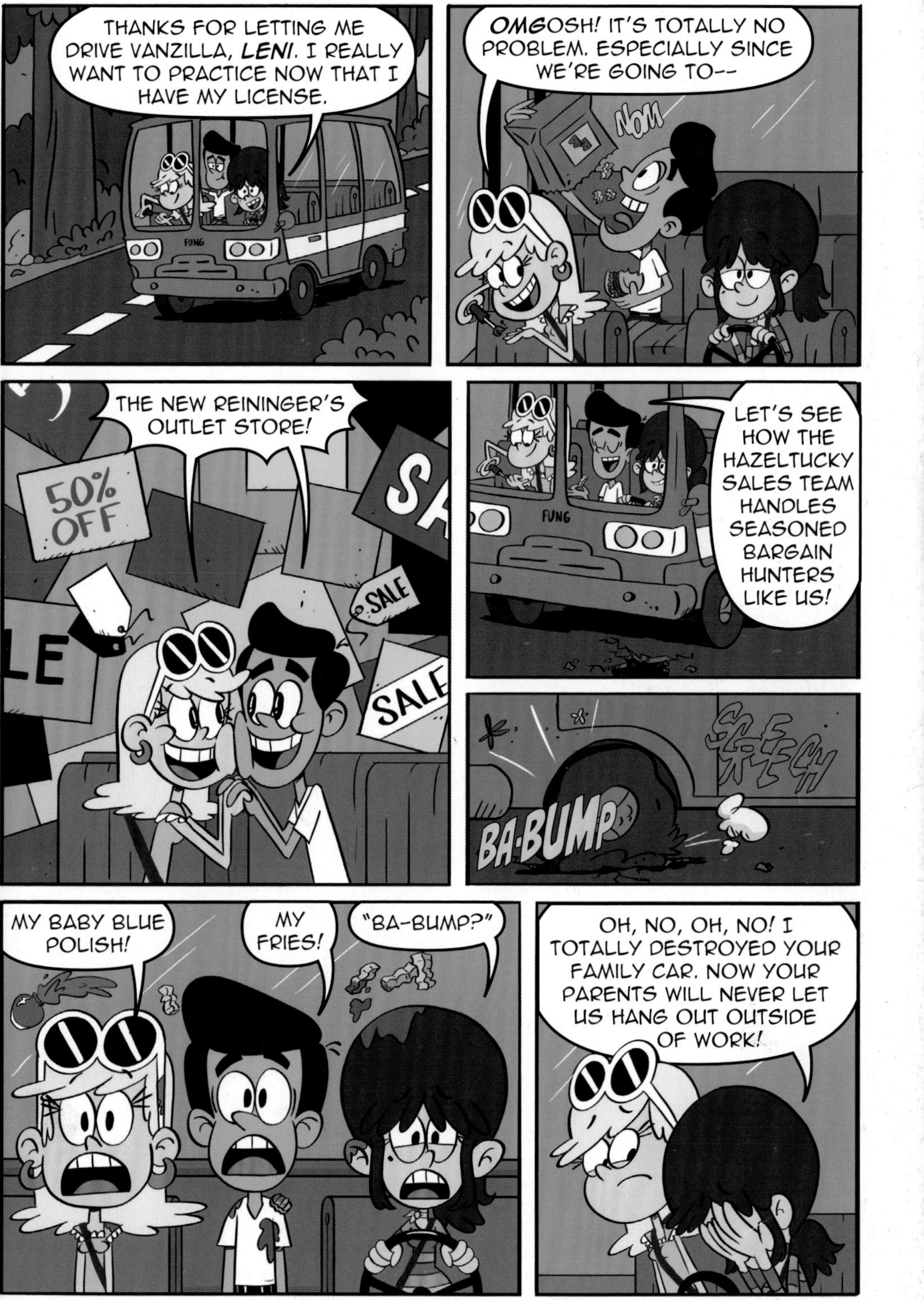
THANKS FOR LETTING ME DRIVE VANZILLA, *LENI*. I REALLY WANT TO PRACTICE NOW THAT I HAVE MY LICENSE.
FUNG
*OMG*OSH! IT'S TOTALLY NO PROBLEM. ESPECIALLY SINCE WE'RE GOING TO--
NOM
THE NEW REININGER'S OUTLET STORE!
50% OFF
SALE
SALE
FUNG
LET'S SEE HOW THE HAZELTUCKY SALES TEAM HANDLES SEASONED BARGAIN HUNTERS LIKE US!
SCREECH
BA-BUMP
MY BABY BLUE POLISH!
MY FRIES!
"BA-BUMP?"
OH, NO, OH, NO! I TOTALLY DESTROYED YOUR FAMILY CAR. NOW YOUR PARENTS WILL NEVER LET US HANG OUT OUTSIDE OF WORK!

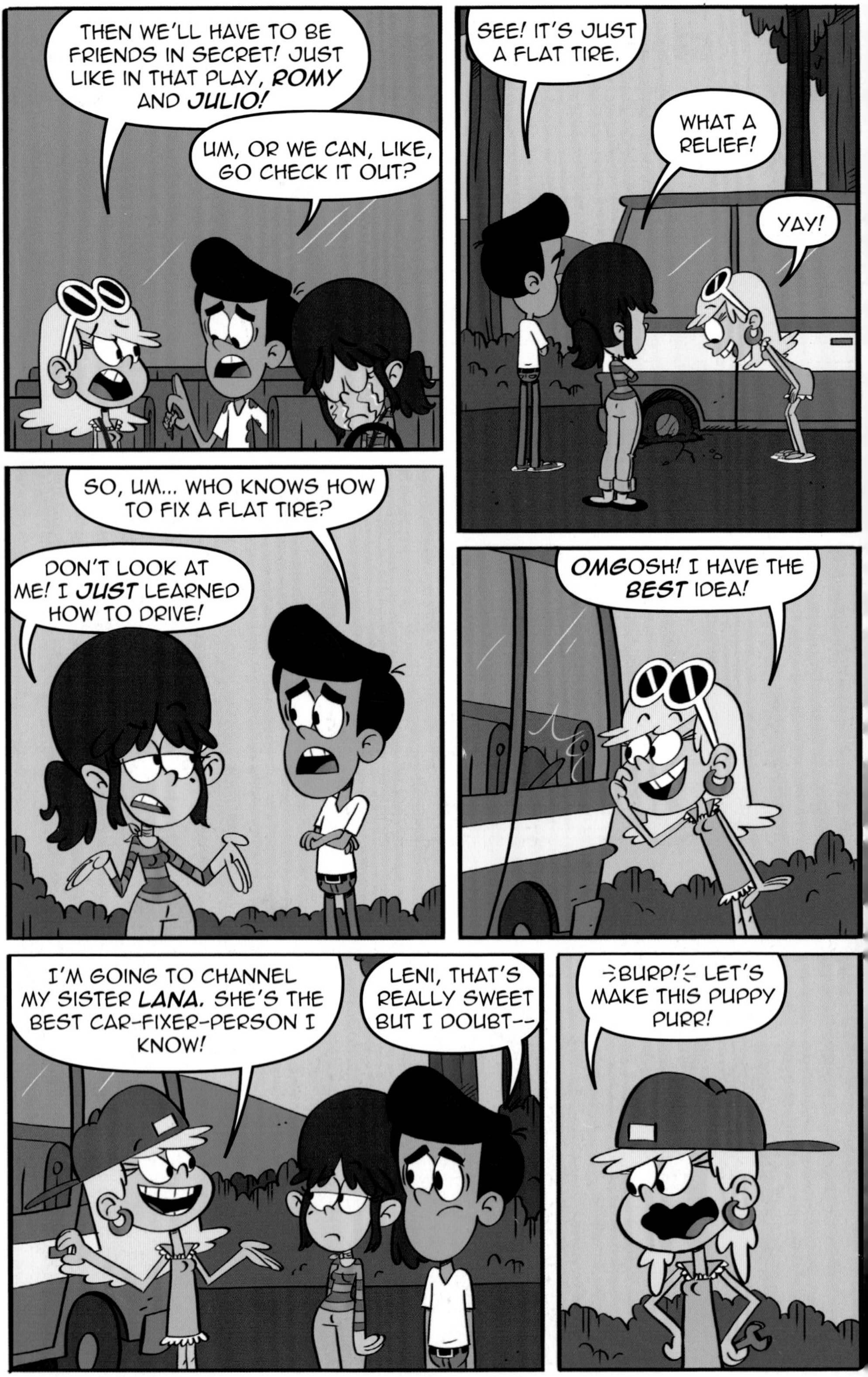
THEN WE'LL HAVE TO BE FRIENDS IN SECRET! JUST LIKE IN THAT PLAY, ROMY AND JULIO!
UM, OR WE CAN, LIKE, GO CHECK IT OUT?
SEE! IT'S JUST A FLAT TIRE.
WHAT A RELIEF!
YAY!
SO, UM... WHO KNOWS HOW TO FIX A FLAT TIRE?
DON'T LOOK AT ME! I JUST LEARNED HOW TO DRIVE!
OMGOSH! I HAVE THE BEST IDEA!
I'M GOING TO CHANNEL MY SISTER LANA. SHE'S THE BEST CAR-FIXER-PERSON I KNOW!
LENI, THAT'S REALLY SWEET BUT I DOUBT--
BURP! LET'S MAKE THIS PUPPY PURR!

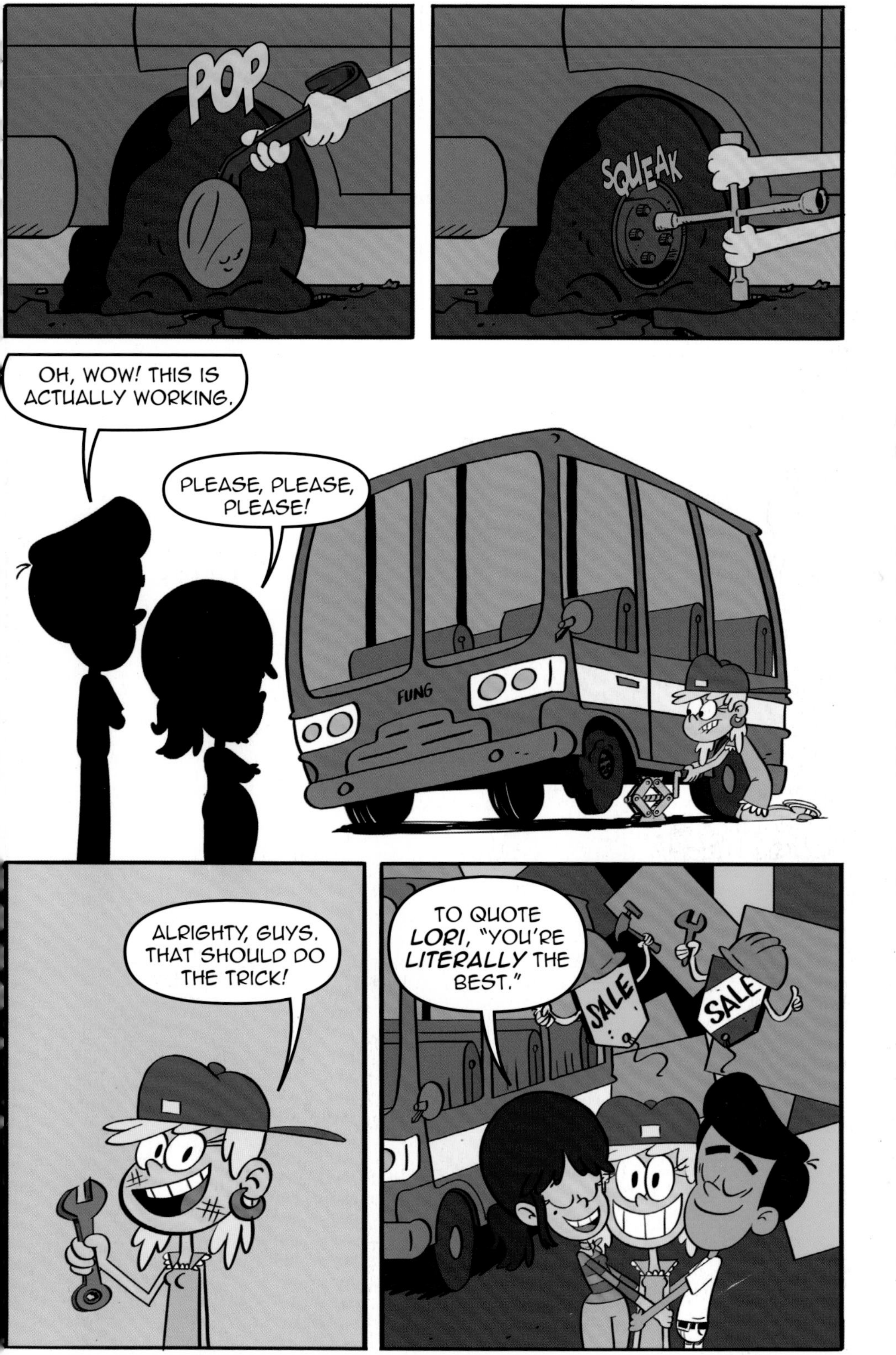
POP
SQUEAK
OH, WOW! THIS IS ACTUALLY WORKING.
PLEASE, PLEASE, PLEASE!
FUNG
ALRIGHTY, GUYS. THAT SHOULD DO THE TRICK!
TO QUOTE LORI, "YOU'RE LITERALLY THE BEST."
SALE
SALE

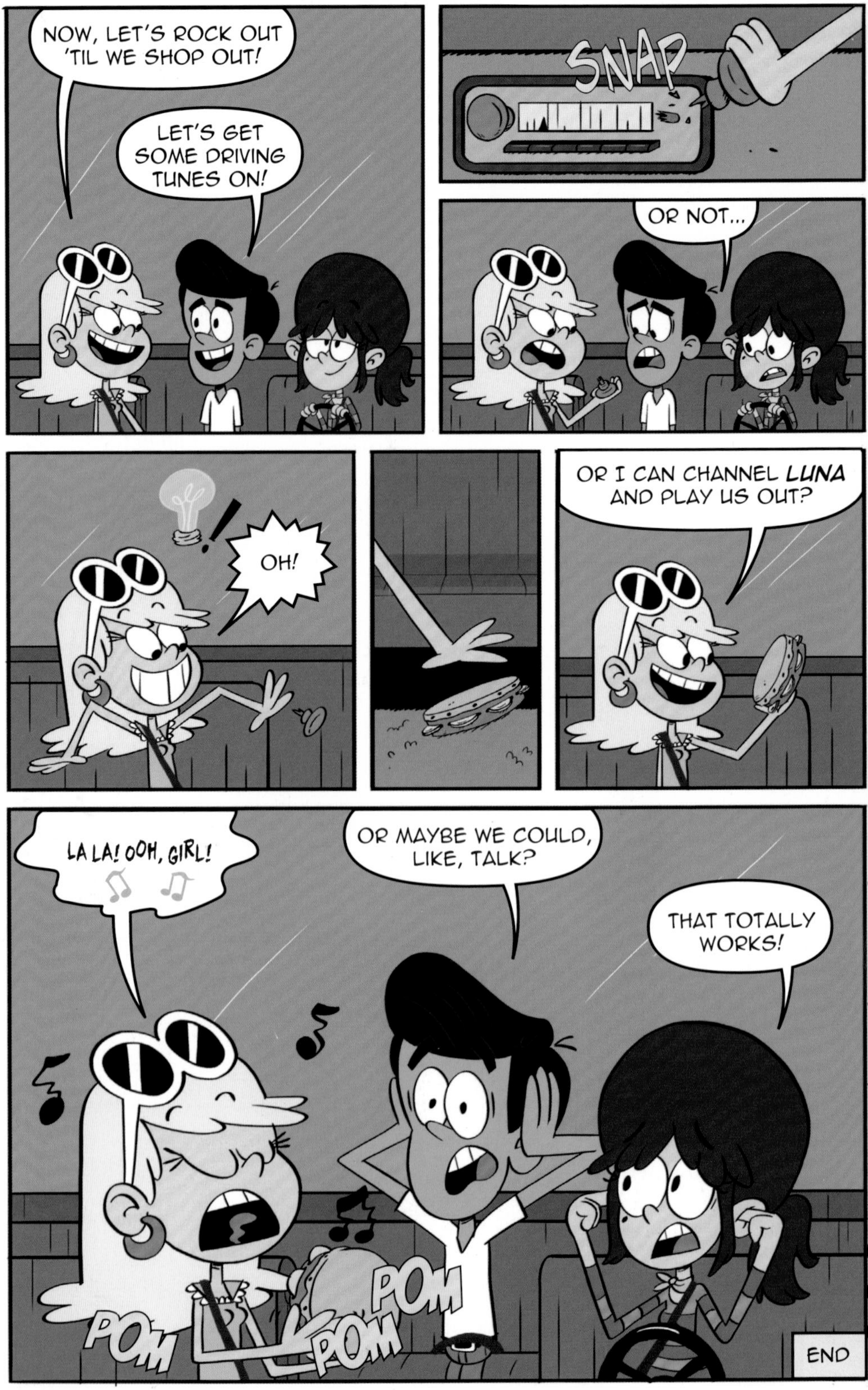
NOW, LET'S ROCK OUT 'TIL WE SHOP OUT!
LET'S GET SOME DRIVING TUNES ON!
SNAP
OR NOT...
OH!
OR I CAN CHANNEL *LUNA* AND PLAY US OUT?
LA LA! OOH, GIRL!
OR MAYBE WE COULD, LIKE, TALK?
THAT TOTALLY WORKS!
POM
POM
POM
END

"HOME SICKNESS!"

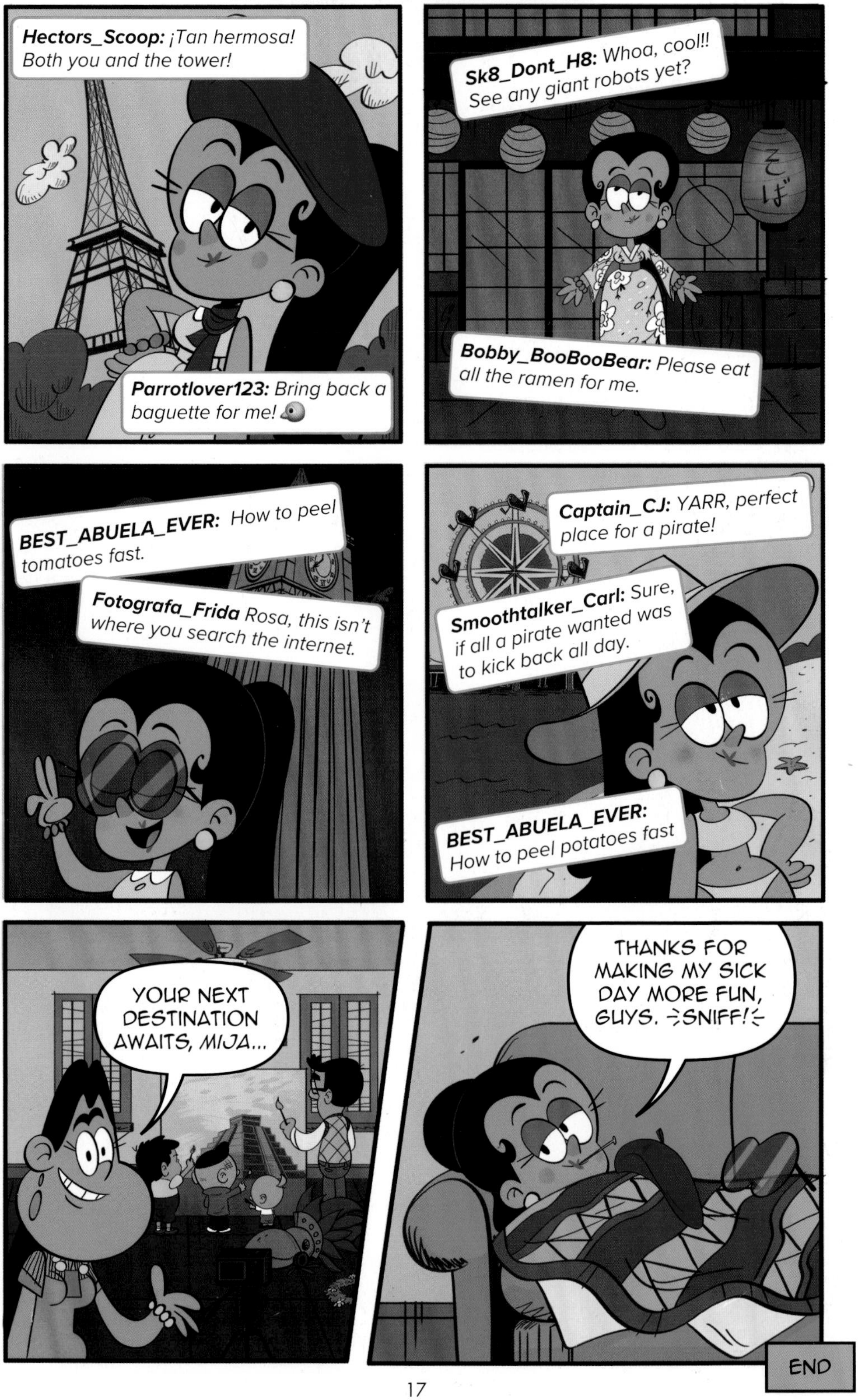
Hectors_Scoop: ¡Tan hermosa! Both you and the tower!
Parrotlover123: Bring back a baguette for me!
Sk8_Dont_H8: Whoa, cool!! See any giant robots yet?
Bobby_BooBooBear: Please eat all the ramen for me.
BEST_ABUELA_EVER: How to peel tomatoes fast.
Fotografa_Frida Rosa, this isn't where you search the internet.
Captain_CJ: YARR, perfect place for a pirate!
Smoothtalker_Carl: Sure, if all a pirate wanted was to kick back all day.
BEST_ABUELA_EVER: How to peel potatoes fast
YOUR NEXT DESTINATION AWAITS, MIJA...
THANKS FOR MAKING MY SICK DAY MORE FUN, GUYS. *SNIFF!*
END

"MUSICAL MYRTLE"

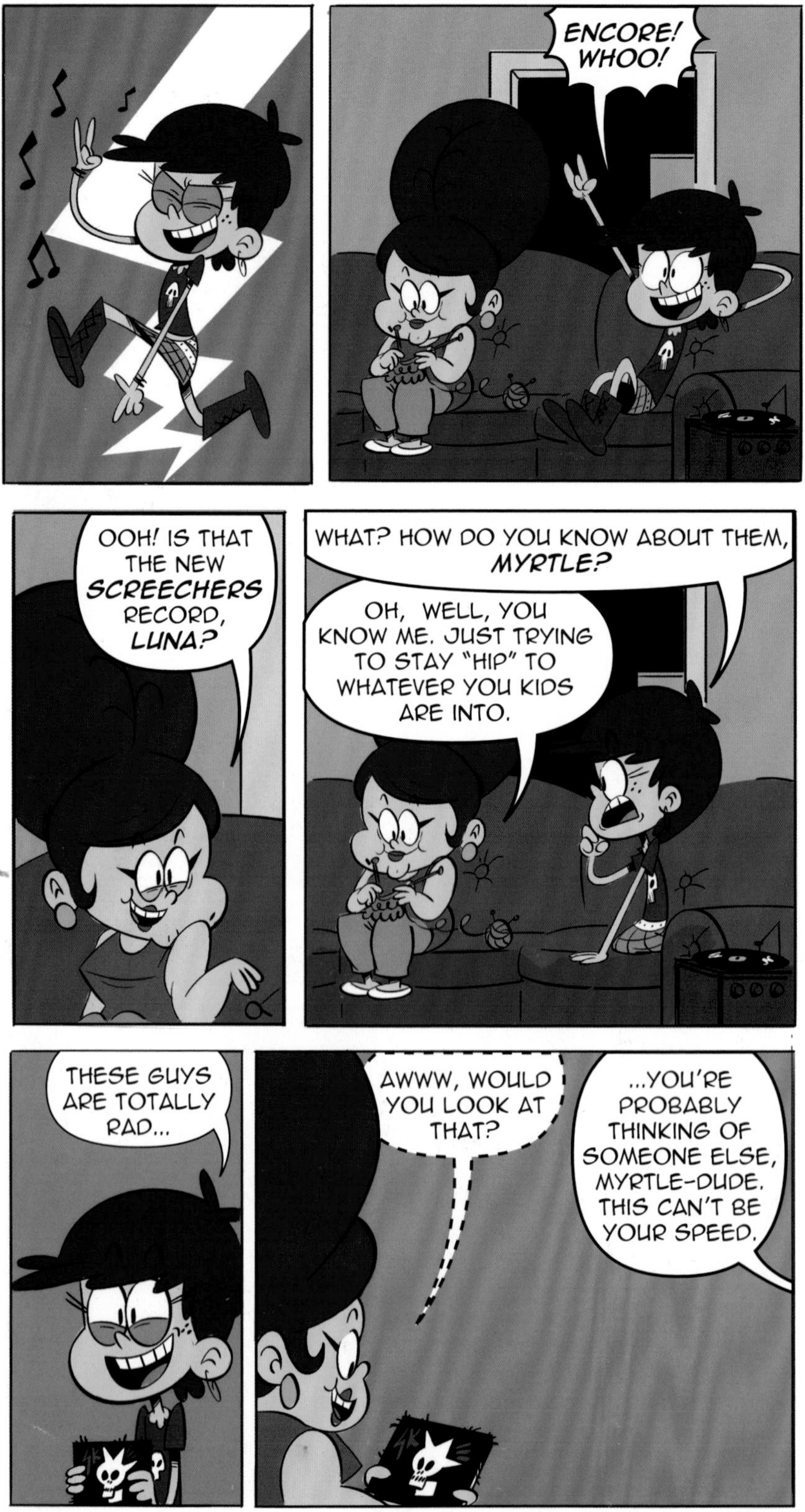
ENCORE! WHOO!
OOH! IS THAT THE NEW SCREECHERS RECORD, LUNA?
WHAT? HOW DO YOU KNOW ABOUT THEM, MYRTLE?
OH, WELL, YOU KNOW ME. JUST TRYING TO STAY "HIP" TO WHATEVER YOU KIDS ARE INTO.
THESE GUYS ARE TOTALLY RAD...
AWWW, WOULD YOU LOOK AT THAT?
...YOU'RE PROBABLY THINKING OF SOMEONE ELSE, MYRTLE-DUDE. THIS CAN'T BE YOUR SPEED.

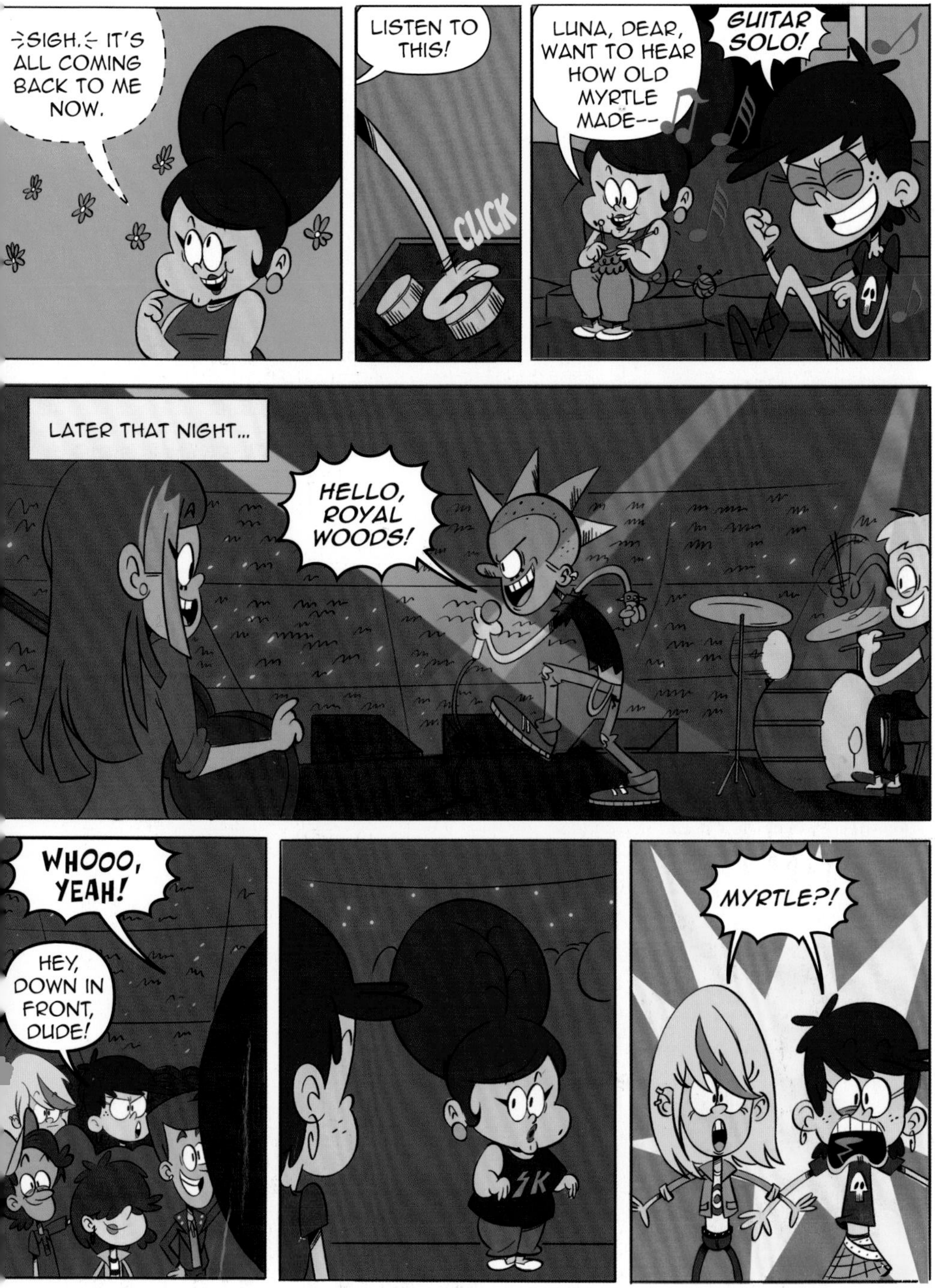

=SIGH.= IT'S ALL COMING BACK TO ME NOW.
LISTEN TO THIS!
CLICK
LUNA, DEAR, WANT TO HEAR HOW OLD MYRTLE MADE--
GUITAR SOLO!
LATER THAT NIGHT...
HELLO, ROYAL WOODS!
WHOOO, YEAH!
HEY, DOWN IN FRONT, DUDE!
MYRTLE?!

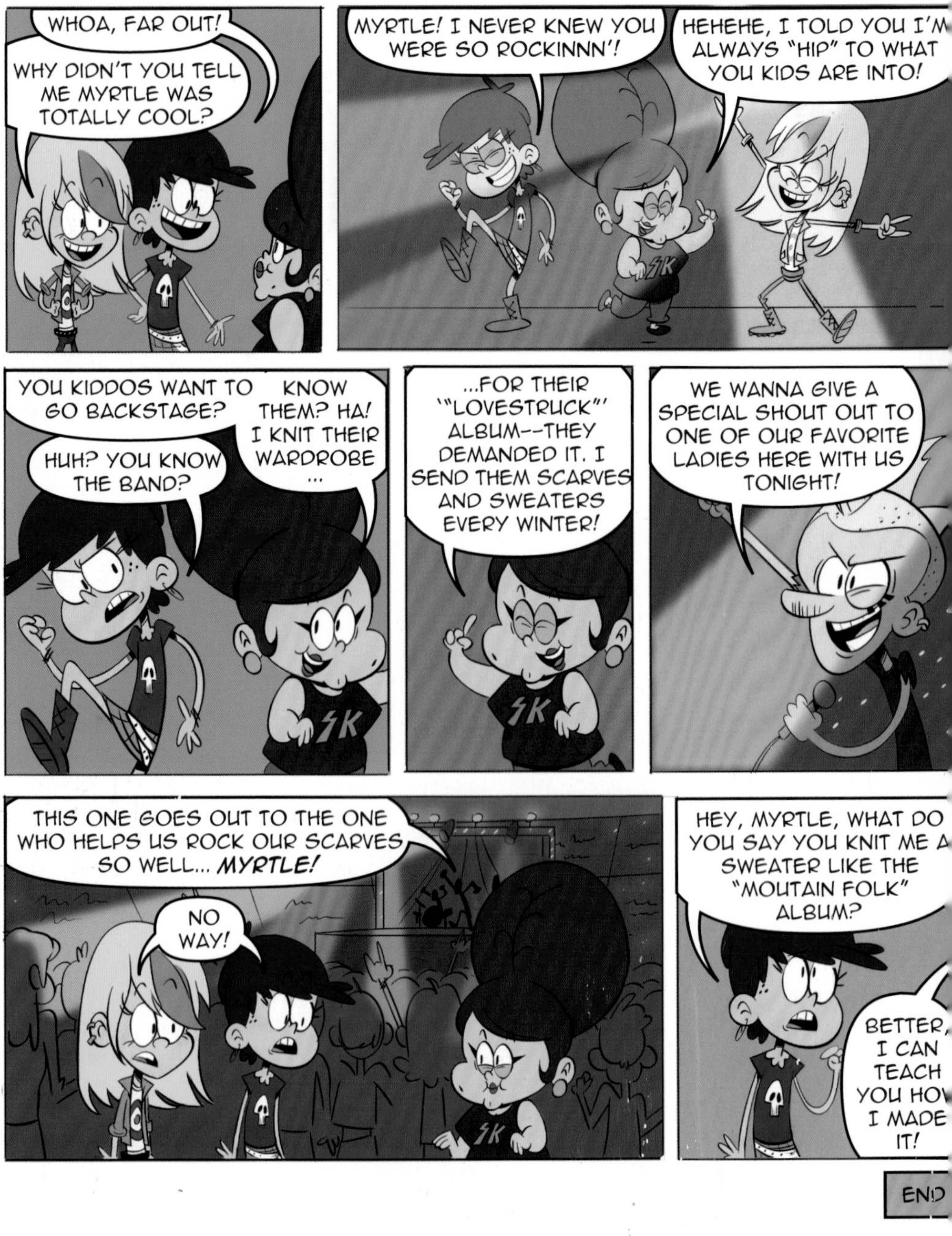
WHOA, FAR OUT!
WHY DIDN'T YOU TELL ME MYRTLE WAS TOTALLY COOL?
MYRTLE! I NEVER KNEW YOU WERE SO ROCKINNN'!
HEHEHE, I TOLD YOU I'M ALWAYS "HIP" TO WHAT YOU KIDS ARE INTO!
YOU KIDDOS WANT TO GO BACKSTAGE?
HUH? YOU KNOW THE BAND?
KNOW THEM? HA! I KNIT THEIR WARDROBE ...
...FOR THEIR '"LOVESTRUCK"' ALBUM--THEY DEMANDED IT. I SEND THEM SCARVES AND SWEATERS EVERY WINTER!
WE WANNA GIVE A SPECIAL SHOUT OUT TO ONE OF OUR FAVORITE LADIES HERE WITH US TONIGHT!
THIS ONE GOES OUT TO THE ONE WHO HELPS US ROCK OUR SCARVES SO WELL... MYRTLE!
NO WAY!
HEY, MYRTLE, WHAT DO YOU SAY YOU KNIT ME A SWEATER LIKE THE "MOUTAIN FOLK" ALBUM?
BETTER, I CAN TEACH YOU HOW I MADE IT!
END

"OCEAN 11"

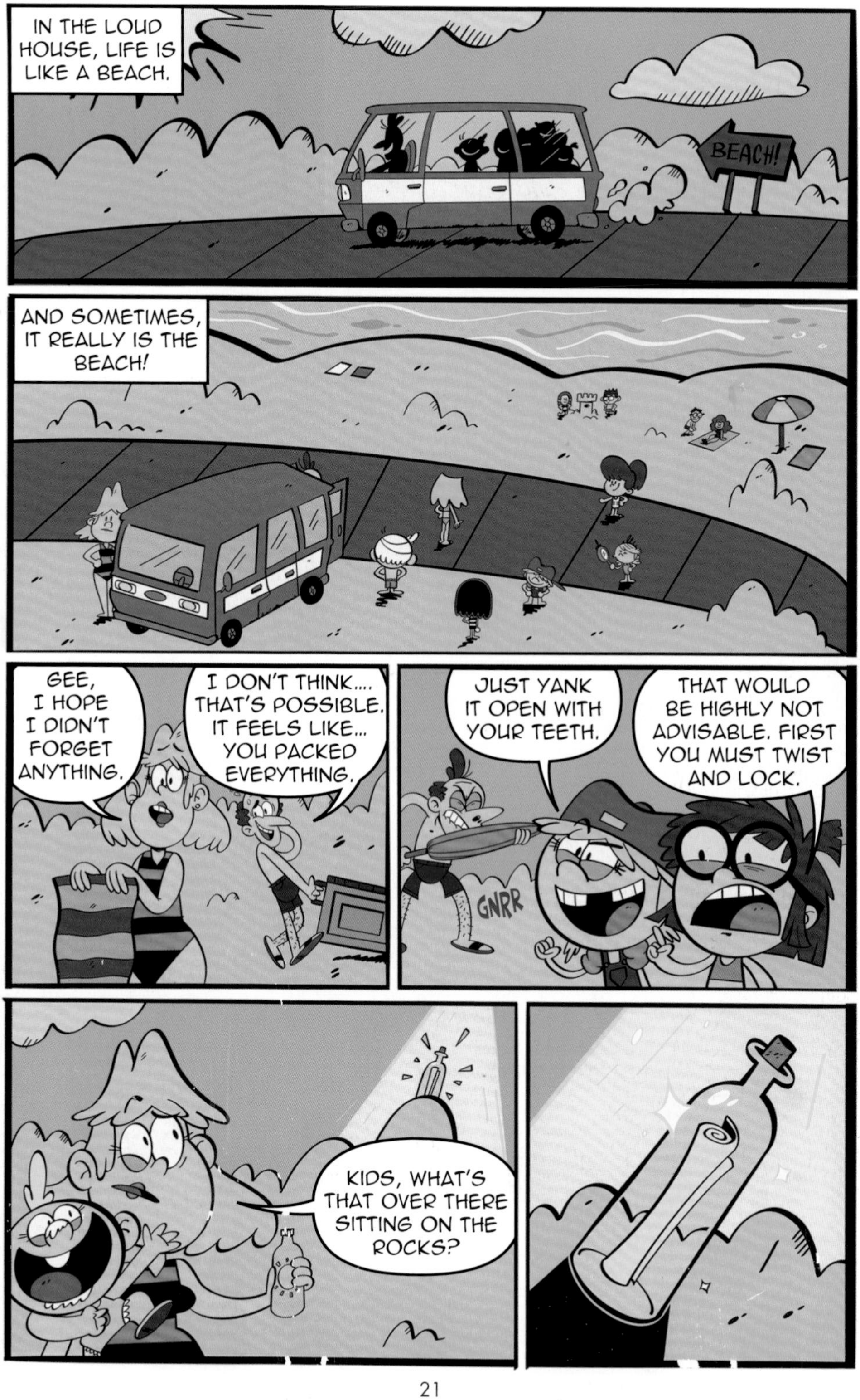

IN THE LOUD HOUSE, LIFE IS LIKE A BEACH.
BEACH!
AND SOMETIMES, IT REALLY IS THE BEACH!
GEE, I HOPE I DIDN'T FORGET ANYTHING.
I DON'T THINK.... THAT'S POSSIBLE. IT FEELS LIKE... YOU PACKED EVERYTHING.
JUST YANK IT OPEN WITH YOUR TEETH.
THAT WOULD BE HIGHLY NOT ADVISABLE. FIRST YOU MUST TWIST AND LOCK.
GNRR
KIDS, WHAT'S THAT OVER THERE SITTING ON THE ROCKS?

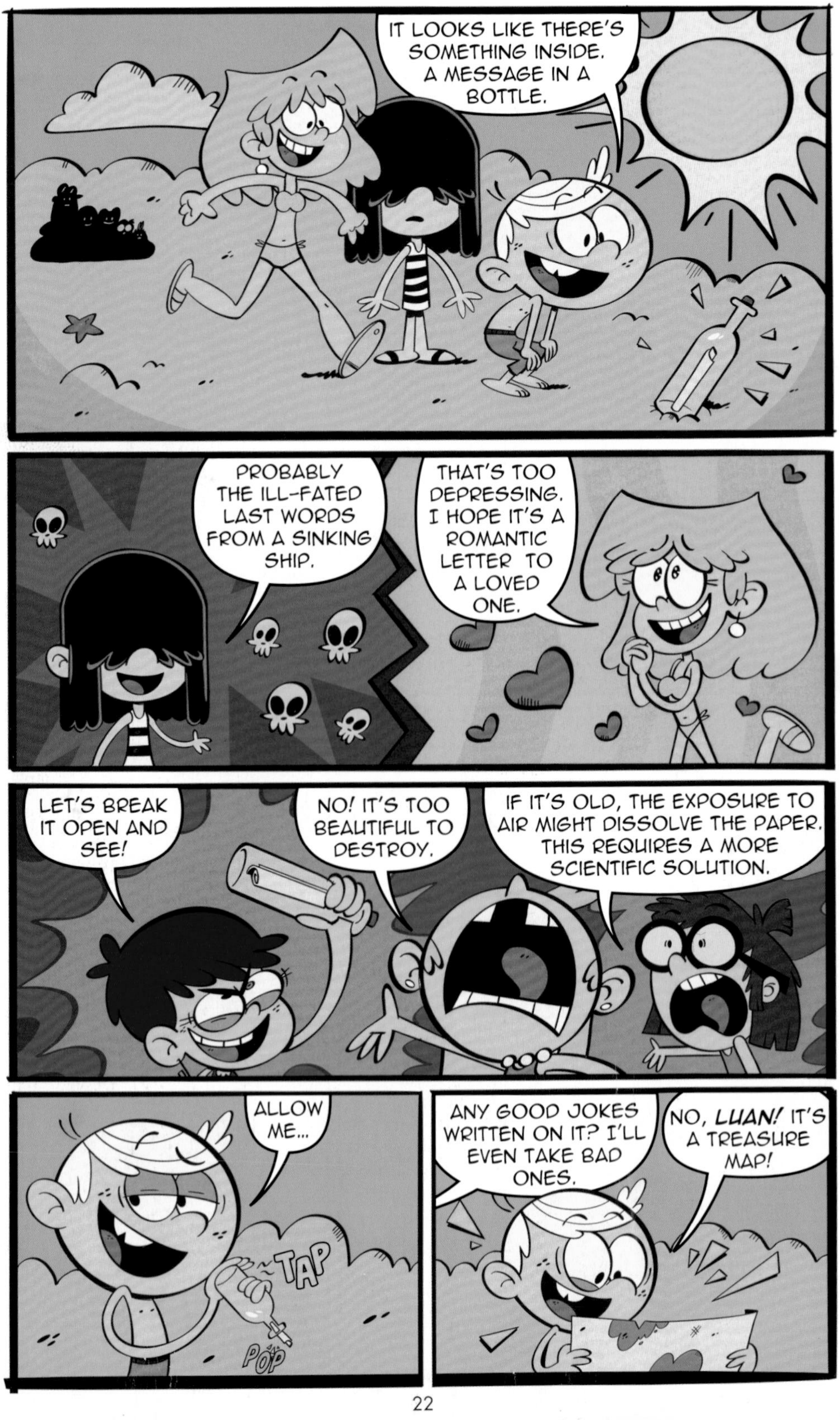
IT LOOKS LIKE THERE'S SOMETHING INSIDE. A MESSAGE IN A BOTTLE.
PROBABLY THE ILL-FATED LAST WORDS FROM A SINKING SHIP.
THAT'S TOO DEPRESSING. I HOPE IT'S A ROMANTIC LETTER TO A LOVED ONE.
LET'S BREAK IT OPEN AND SEE!
NO! IT'S TOO BEAUTIFUL TO DESTROY.
IF IT'S OLD, THE EXPOSURE TO AIR MIGHT DISSOLVE THE PAPER. THIS REQUIRES A MORE SCIENTIFIC SOLUTION.
ALLOW ME...
TAP
POP
ANY GOOD JOKES WRITTEN ON IT? I'LL EVEN TAKE BAD ONES.
NO, **LUAN!** IT'S A TREASURE MAP!

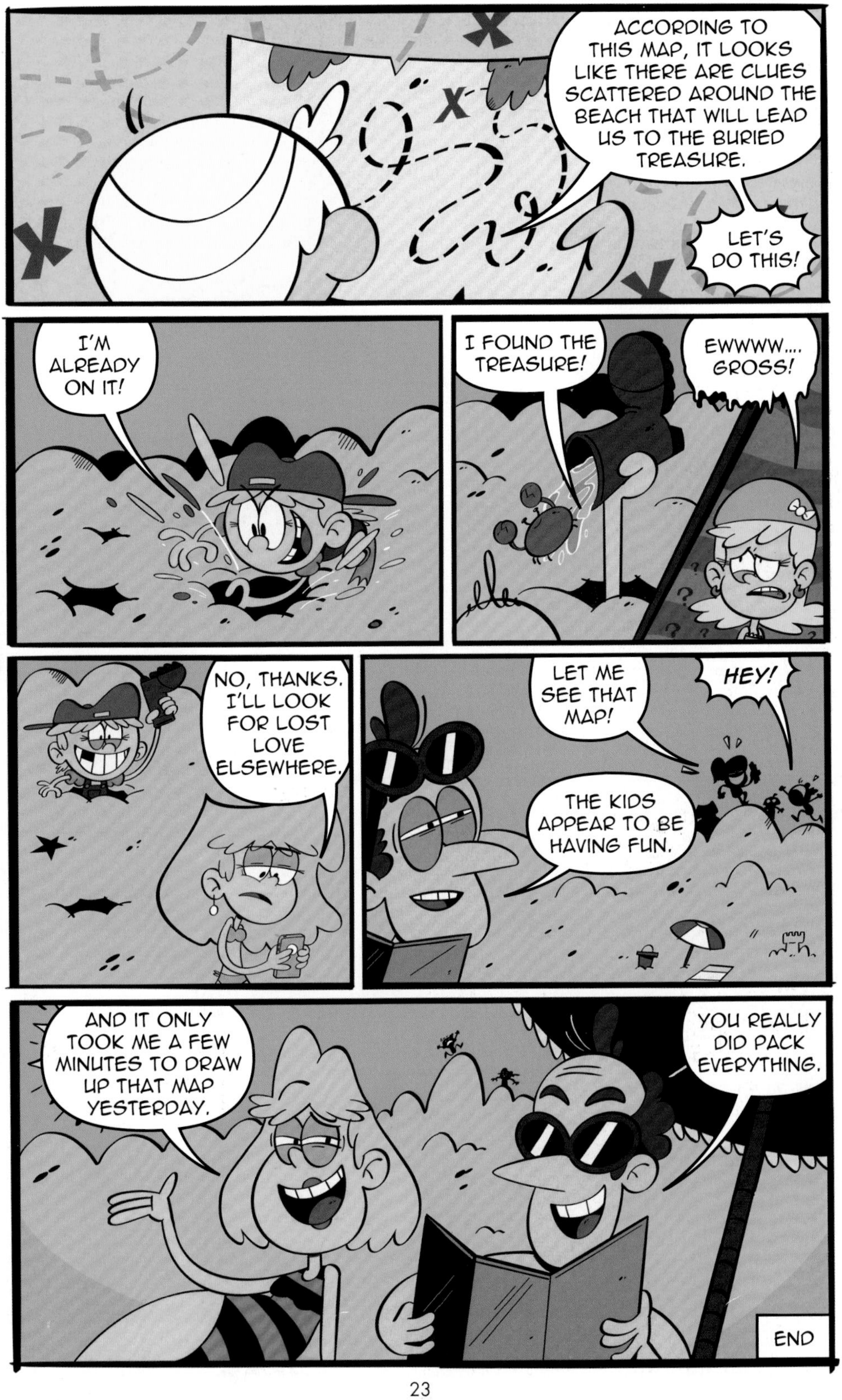
ACCORDING TO THIS MAP, IT LOOKS LIKE THERE ARE CLUES SCATTERED AROUND THE BEACH THAT WILL LEAD US TO THE BURIED TREASURE.
LET'S DO THIS!
I'M ALREADY ON IT!
I FOUND THE TREASURE!
EWWWW.... GROSS!
NO, THANKS. I'LL LOOK FOR LOST LOVE ELSEWHERE.
LET ME SEE THAT MAP!
HEY!
THE KIDS APPEAR TO BE HAVING FUN.
AND IT ONLY TOOK ME A FEW MINUTES TO DRAW UP THAT MAP YESTERDAY.
YOU REALLY DID PACK EVERYTHING.
END

"FREE TO BE ME"

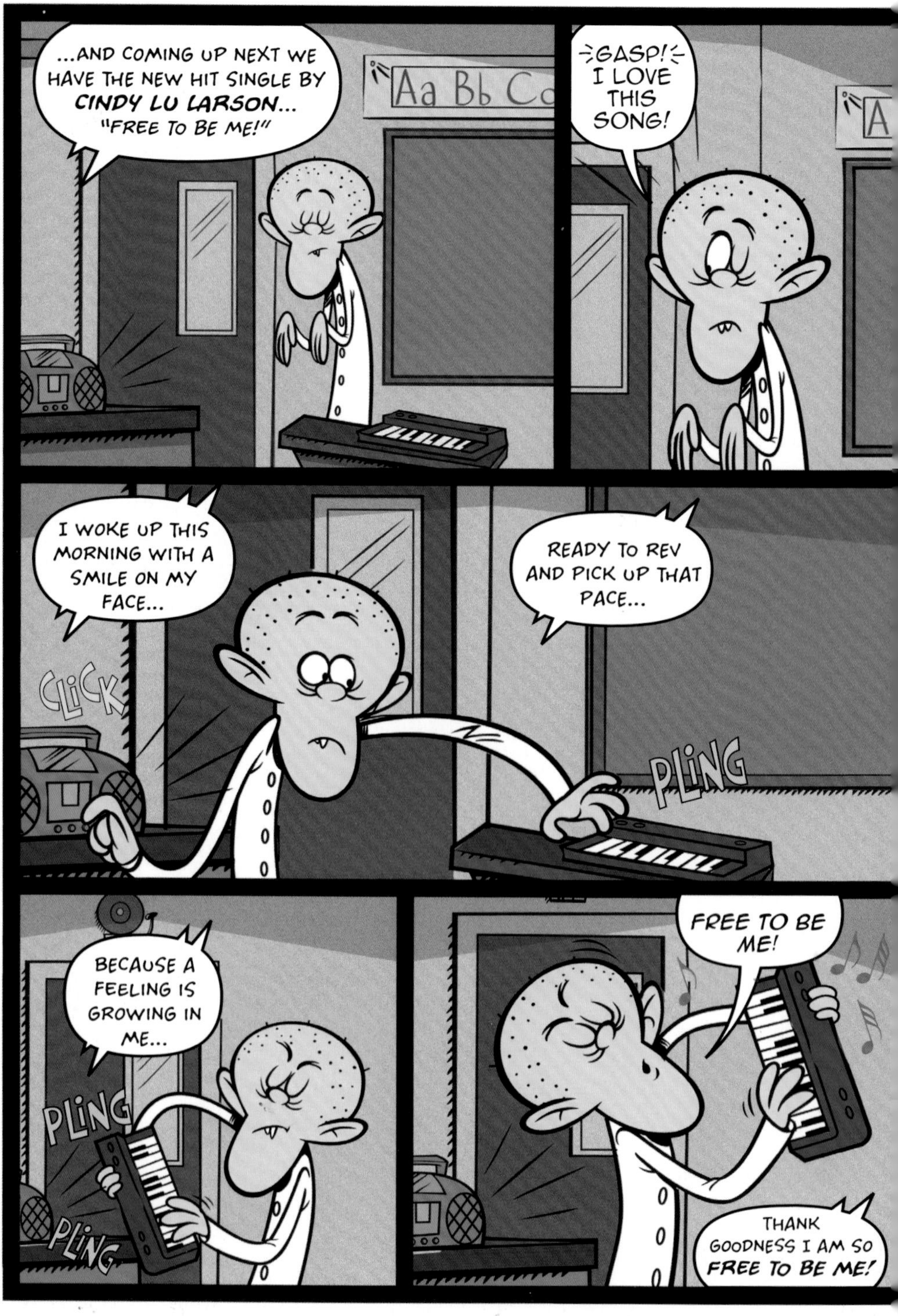

...AND COMING UP NEXT WE HAVE THE NEW HIT SINGLE BY CINDY LU LARSON... "FREE TO BE ME!"
Aa Bb Cc
GASP! I LOVE THIS SONG!
I WOKE UP THIS MORNING WITH A SMILE ON MY FACE...
CLICK
READY TO REV AND PICK UP THAT PACE...
PLING
BECAUSE A FEELING IS GROWING IN ME...
PLING
PLING
FREE TO BE ME!
THANK GOODNESS I AM SO FREE TO BE ME!

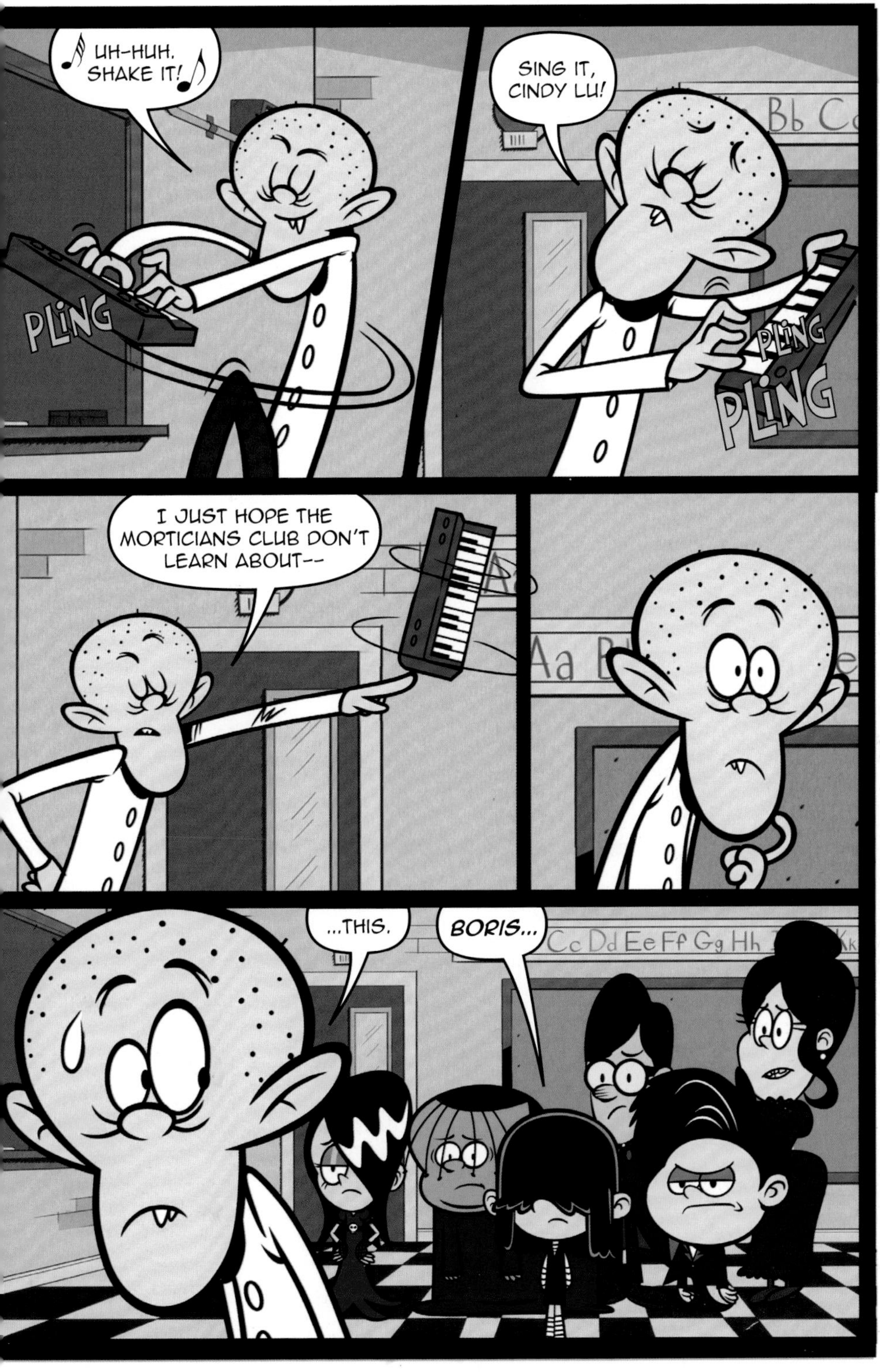
UH-HUH. SHAKE IT!
PLING
SING IT, CINDY LU!
PLING
PLING
Bb Cc
I JUST HOPE THE MORTICIANS CLUB DON'T LEARN ABOUT--
Aa
...THIS.
BORIS...
Cc Dd Ee Ff Gg Hh

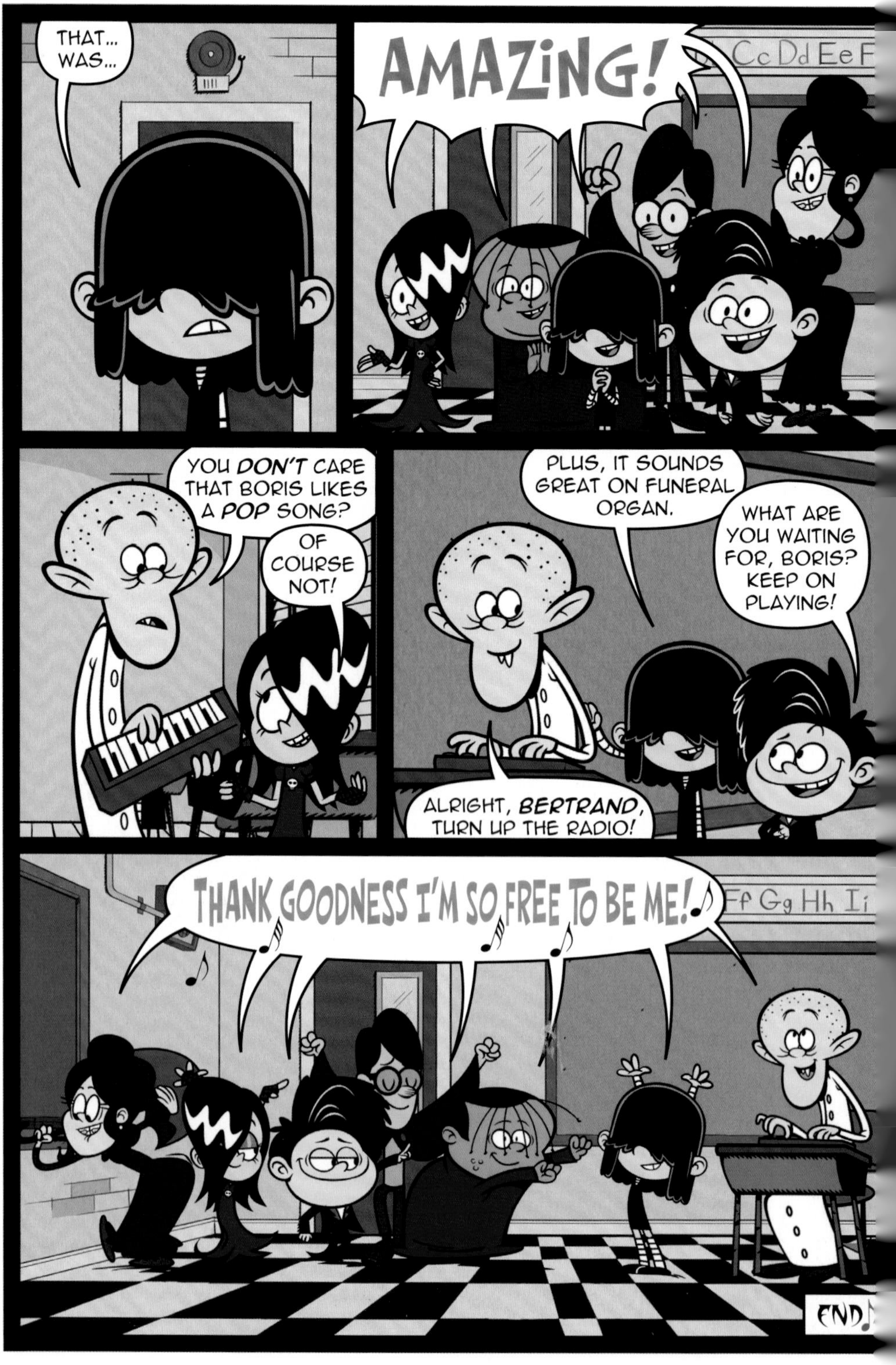
THAT... WAS...
AMAZING!
YOU DON'T CARE THAT BORIS LIKES A POP SONG?
OF COURSE NOT!
PLUS, IT SOUNDS GREAT ON FUNERAL ORGAN.
WHAT ARE YOU WAITING FOR, BORIS? KEEP ON PLAYING!
ALRIGHT, BERTRAND, TURN UP THE RADIO!
THANK GOODNESS I'M SO FREE TO BE ME!
END

"SNACK ATTACK"

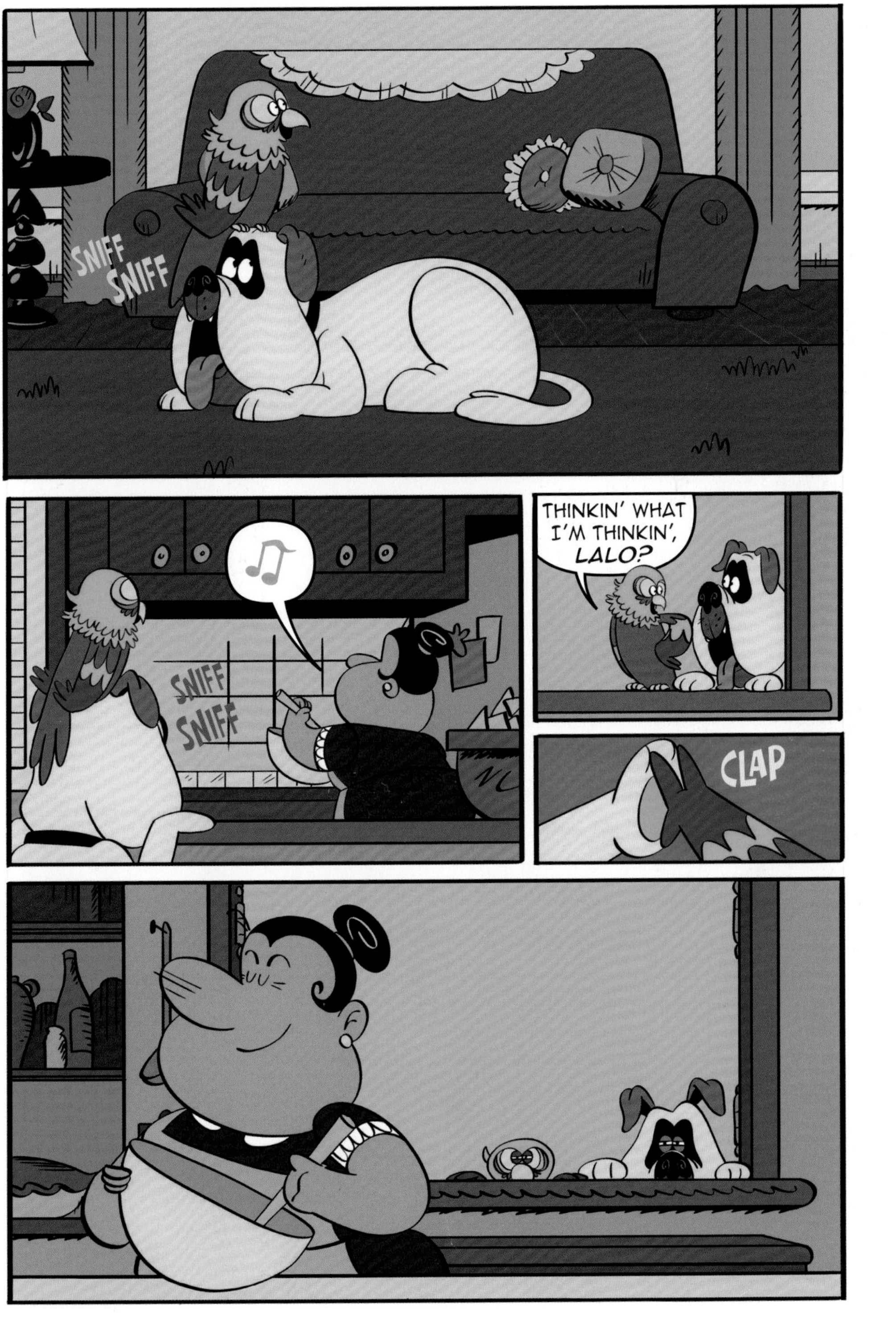
SNIFF SNIFF
SNIFF SNIFF
THINKIN' WHAT I'M THINKIN', LALO?
CLAP

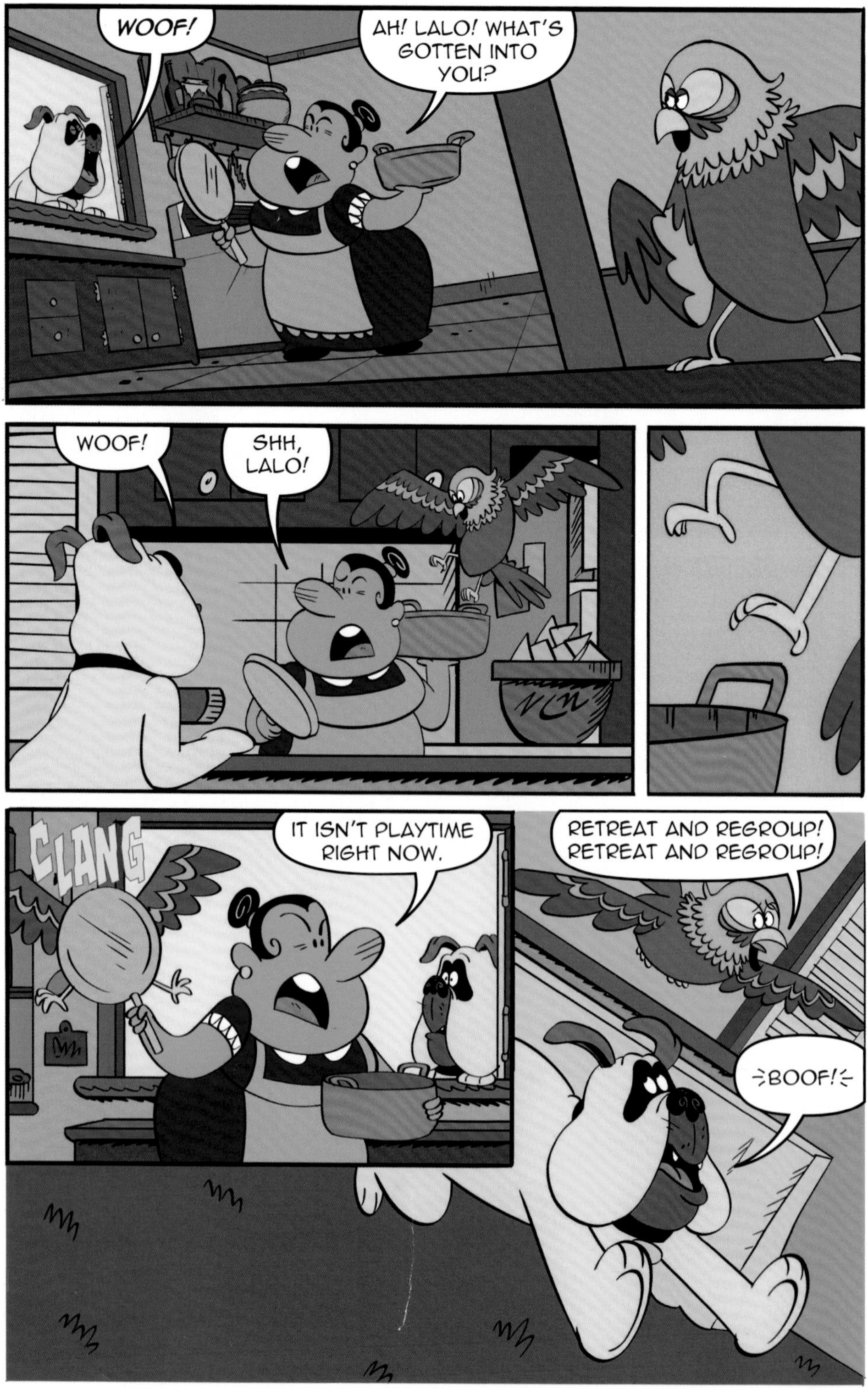
WOOF!
AH! LALO! WHAT'S GOTTEN INTO YOU?
WOOF!
SHH, LALO!
CLANG
IT ISN'T PLAYTIME RIGHT NOW.
RETREAT AND REGROUP! RETREAT AND REGROUP!
BOOF!

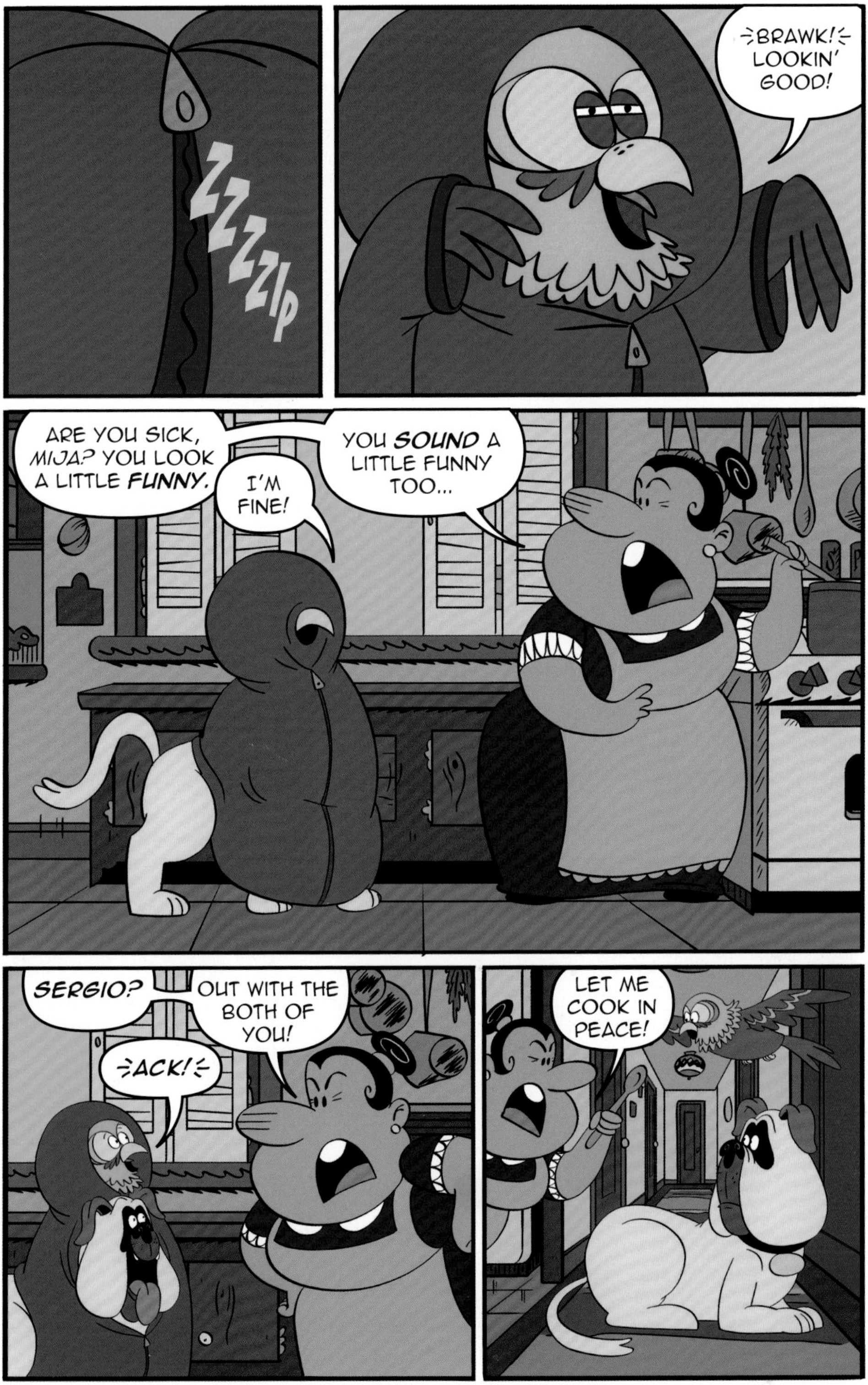

ZZZZZIP
BRAWK! LOOKIN' GOOD!
ARE YOU SICK, MIJA? YOU LOOK A LITTLE FUNNY.
I'M FINE!
YOU SOUND A LITTLE FUNNY TOO...
SERGIO?
OUT WITH THE BOTH OF YOU!
ACK!
LET ME COOK IN PEACE!

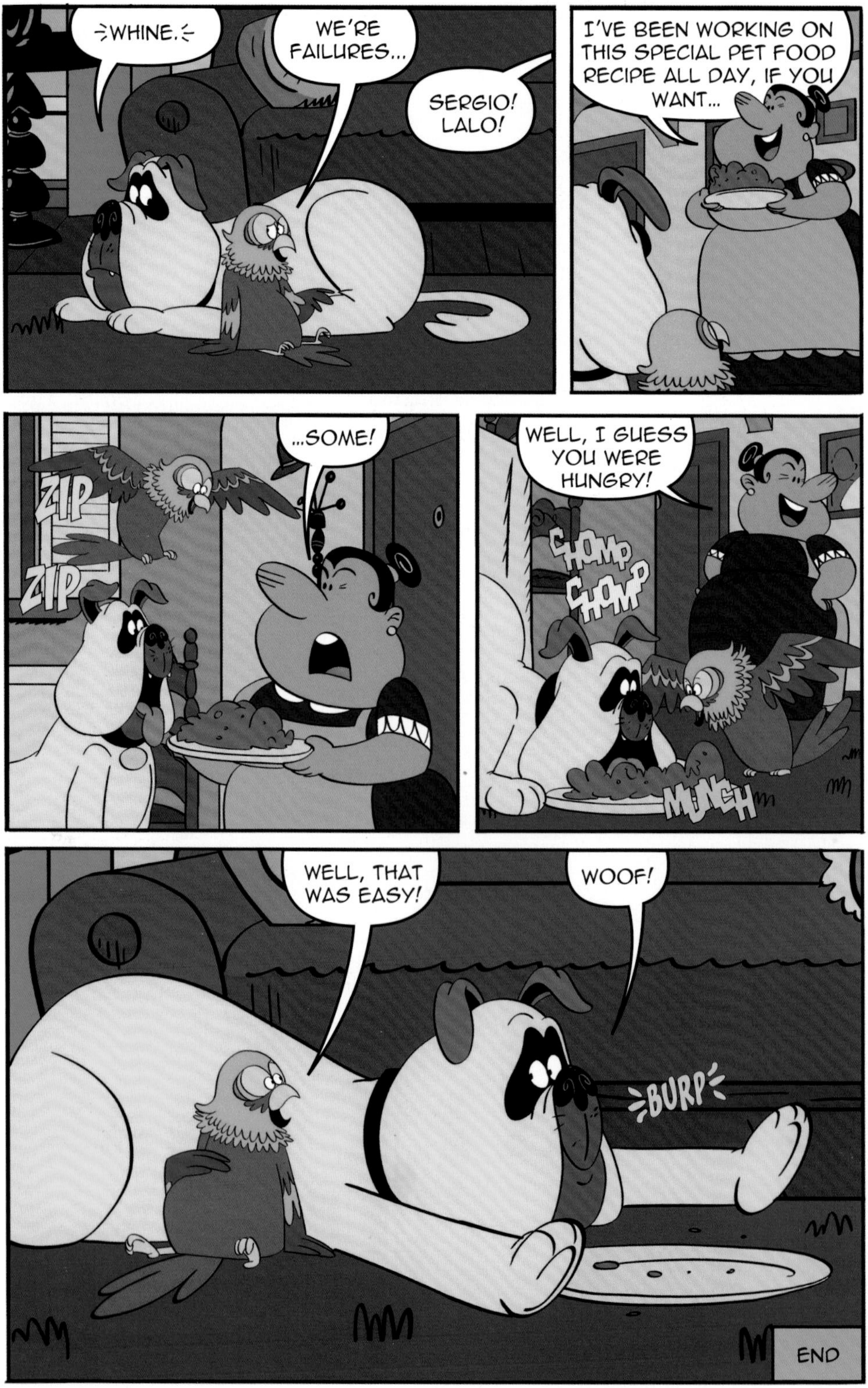
WHINE.
WE'RE FAILURES...
SERGIO! LALO!
I'VE BEEN WORKING ON THIS SPECIAL PET FOOD RECIPE ALL DAY, IF YOU WANT...
ZIP
ZIP
...SOME!
WELL, I GUESS YOU WERE HUNGRY!
CHOMP
CHOMP
MUNCH
WELL, THAT WAS EASY!
WOOF!
BURP
END

"THAT'S A WRAP"

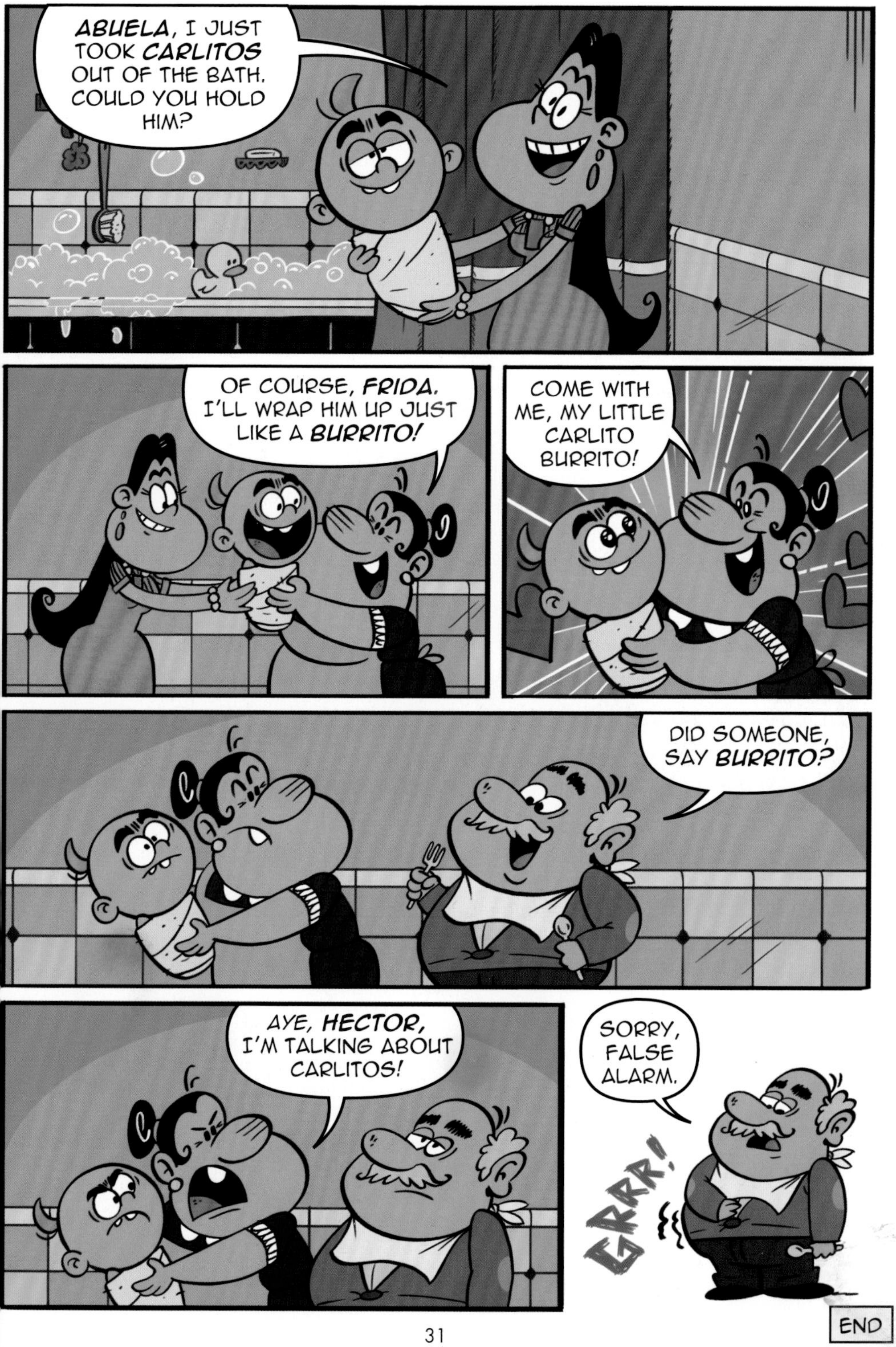
ABUELA, I JUST TOOK CARLITOS OUT OF THE BATH. COULD YOU HOLD HIM?
OF COURSE, FRIDA. I'LL WRAP HIM UP JUST LIKE A BURRITO!
COME WITH ME, MY LITTLE CARLITO BURRITO!
DID SOMEONE, SAY BURRITO?
AYE, HECTOR, I'M TALKING ABOUT CARLITOS!
SORRY, FALSE ALARM.
GRRR!
END

"MACABRE MUNCHIES"

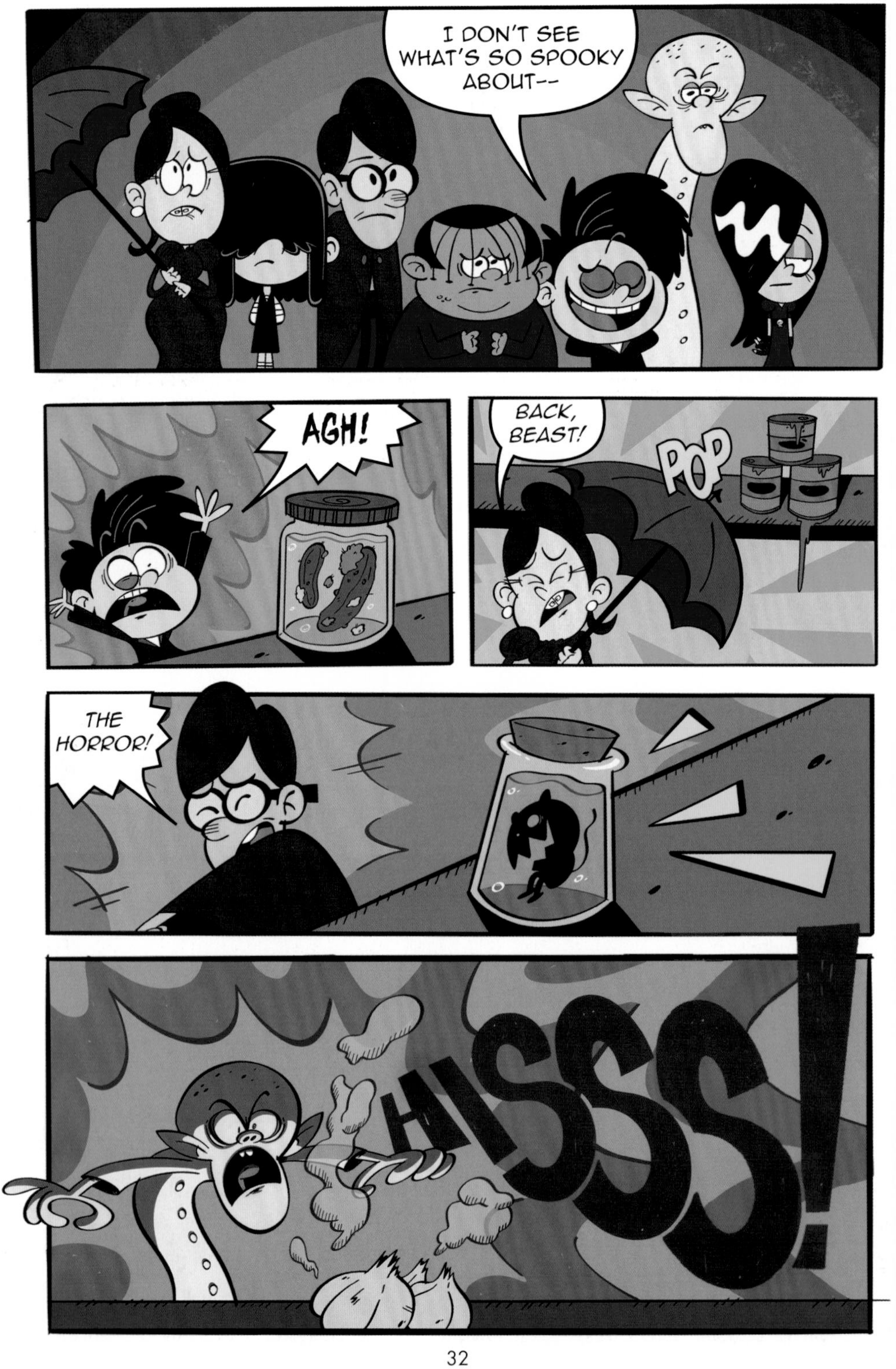
I DON'T SEE WHAT'S SO SPOOKY ABOUT--
AGH!
BACK, BEAST!
POP
THE HORROR!
HISSS!

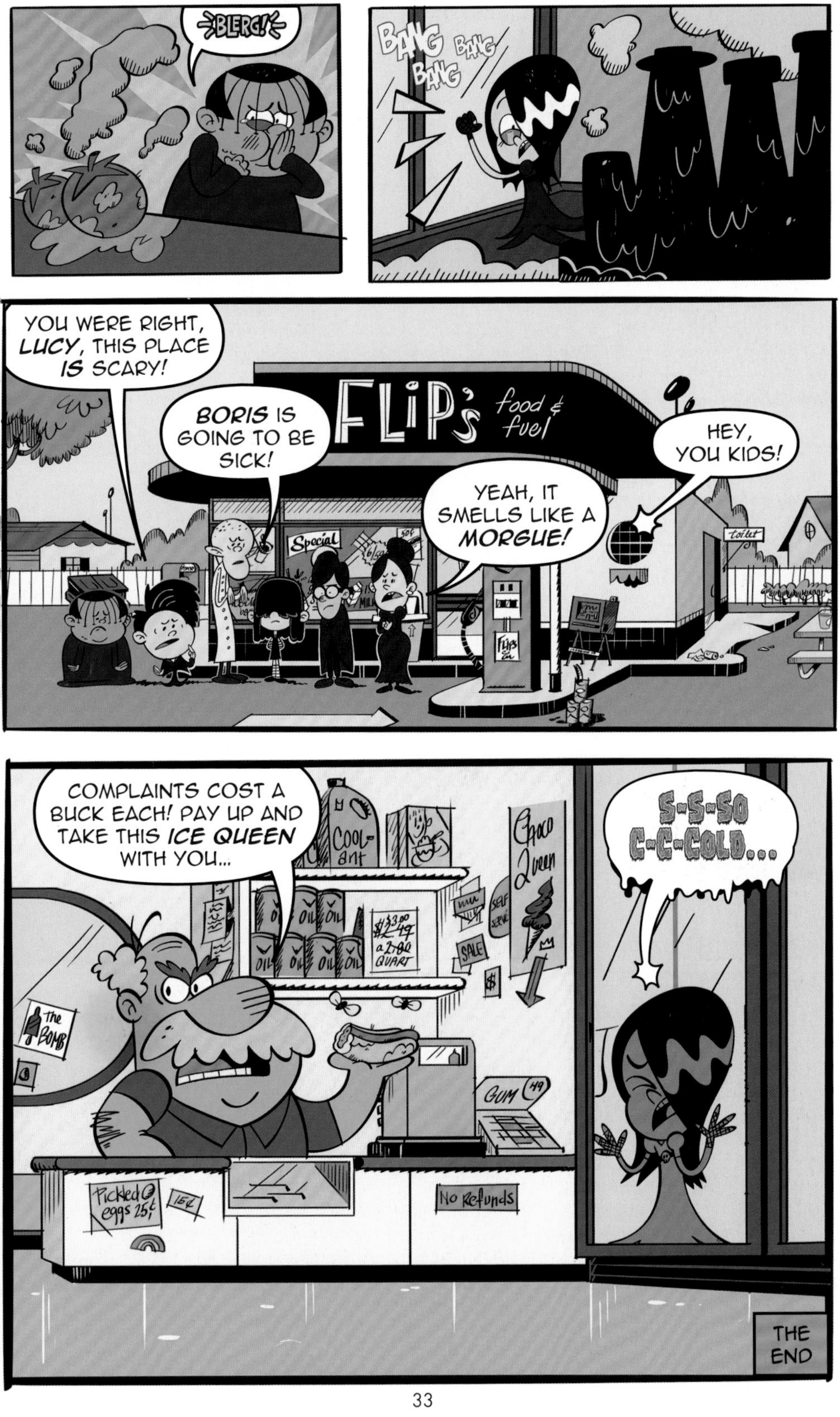
BLERG!
BANG BANG BANG
YOU WERE RIGHT, LUCY, THIS PLACE IS SCARY!
BORIS IS GOING TO BE SICK!
FLIP's food & fuel
YEAH, IT SMELLS LIKE A MORGUE!
HEY, YOU KIDS!
Special
toilet
COMPLAINTS COST A BUCK EACH! PAY UP AND TAKE THIS ICE QUEEN WITH YOU...
S-S-SO C-C-COLD...
COOL-ant
Choco Queen
OIL
SALE
The BOMB
GUM 49
Pickled eggs 25¢
15¢
No Refunds
THE END

"CANNONBALL RUN"

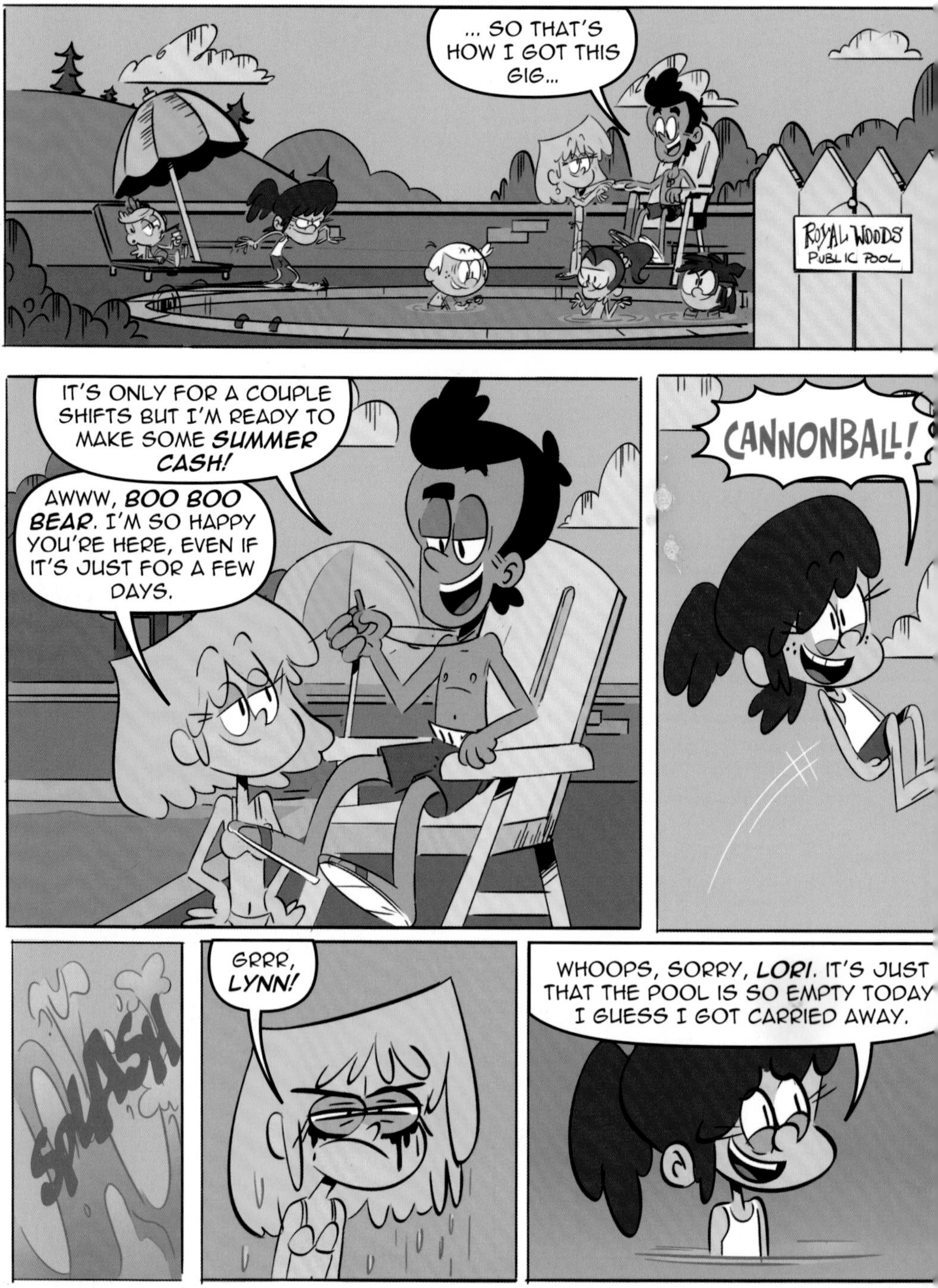
... SO THAT'S HOW I GOT THIS GIG...
ROYAL WOODS PUBLIC POOL
IT'S ONLY FOR A COUPLE SHIFTS BUT I'M READY TO MAKE SOME *SUMMER CASH!*
AWWW, *BOO BOO BEAR*. I'M SO HAPPY YOU'RE HERE, EVEN IF IT'S JUST FOR A FEW DAYS.
CANNONBALL!
SPLASH
GRRR, *LYNN!*
WHOOPS, SORRY, *LORI*. IT'S JUST THAT THE POOL IS SO EMPTY TODAY I GUESS I GOT CARRIED AWAY.

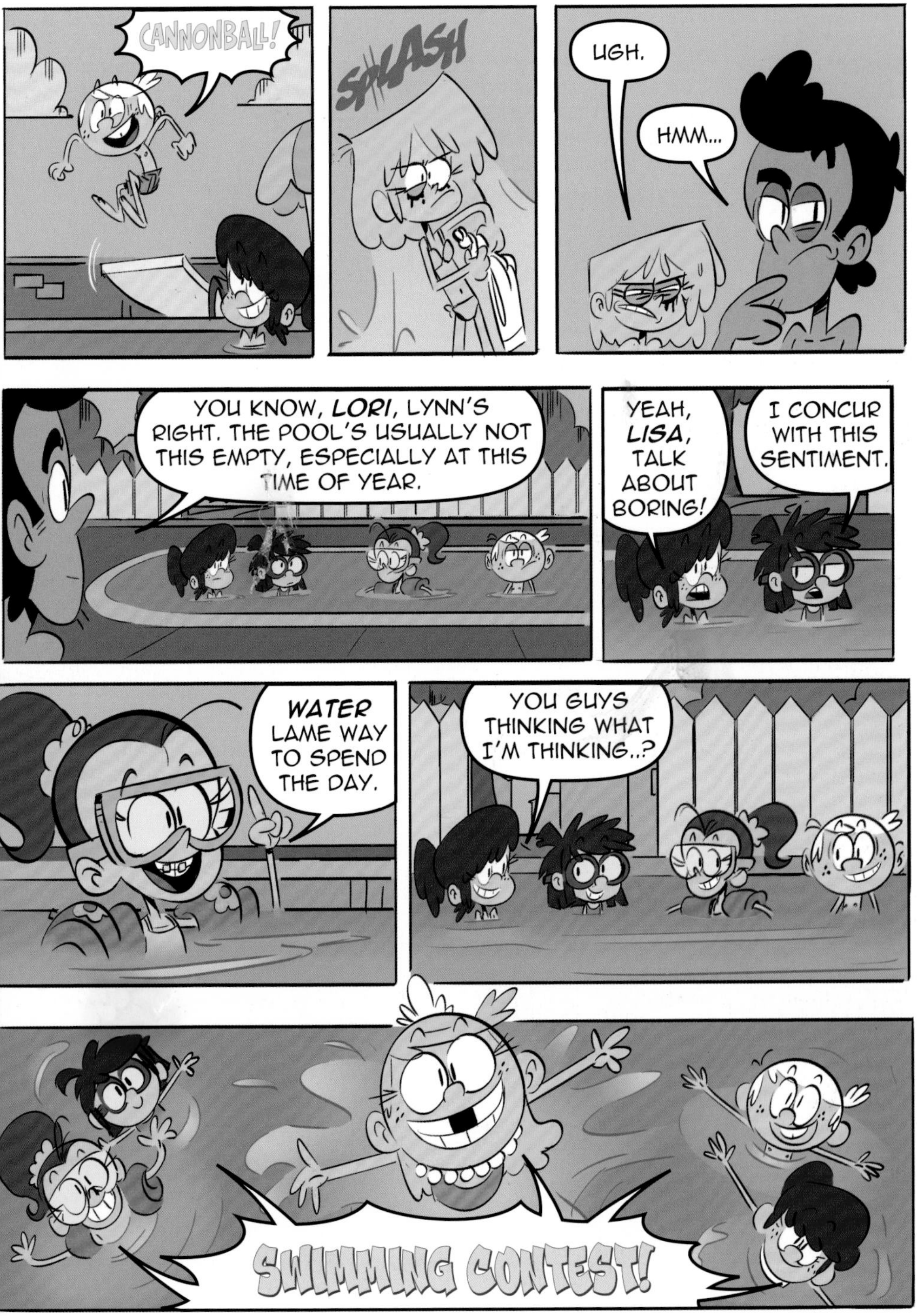
CANNONBALL!
SPLASH
UGH.
HMM...
YOU KNOW, LORI, LYNN'S RIGHT. THE POOL'S USUALLY NOT THIS EMPTY, ESPECIALLY AT THIS TIME OF YEAR.
YEAH, LISA, TALK ABOUT BORING!
I CONCUR WITH THIS SENTIMENT.
WATER LAME WAY TO SPEND THE DAY.
YOU GUYS THINKING WHAT I'M THINKING..?
SWIMMING CONTEST!

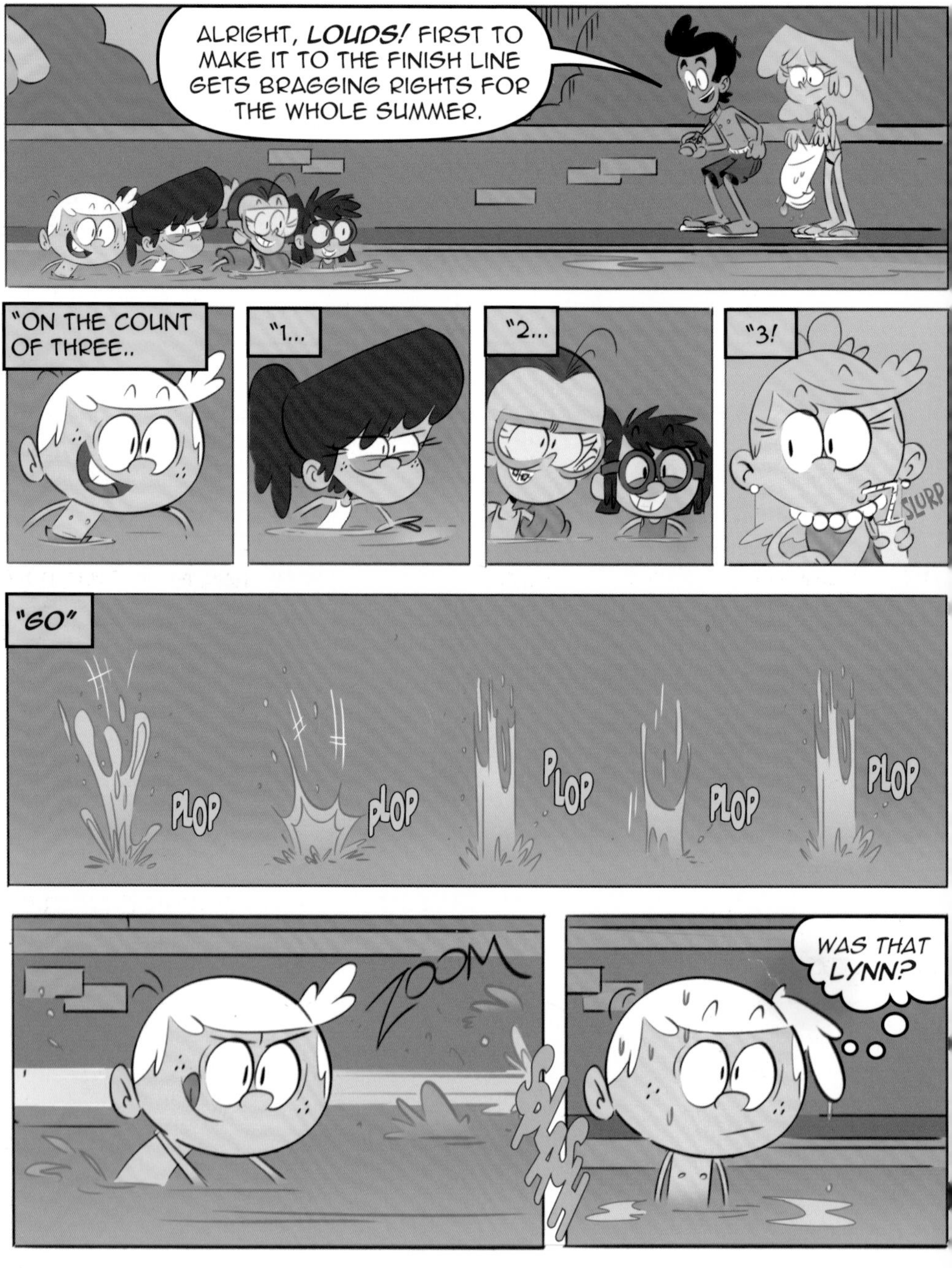
ALRIGHT, LOUDS! FIRST TO MAKE IT TO THE FINISH LINE GETS BRAGGING RIGHTS FOR THE WHOLE SUMMER.
"ON THE COUNT OF THREE..
"1...
"2...
"3!
SLURP
"GO"
PLOP
PLOP
PLOP
PLOP
PLOP
ZOOM
WAS THAT LYNN?

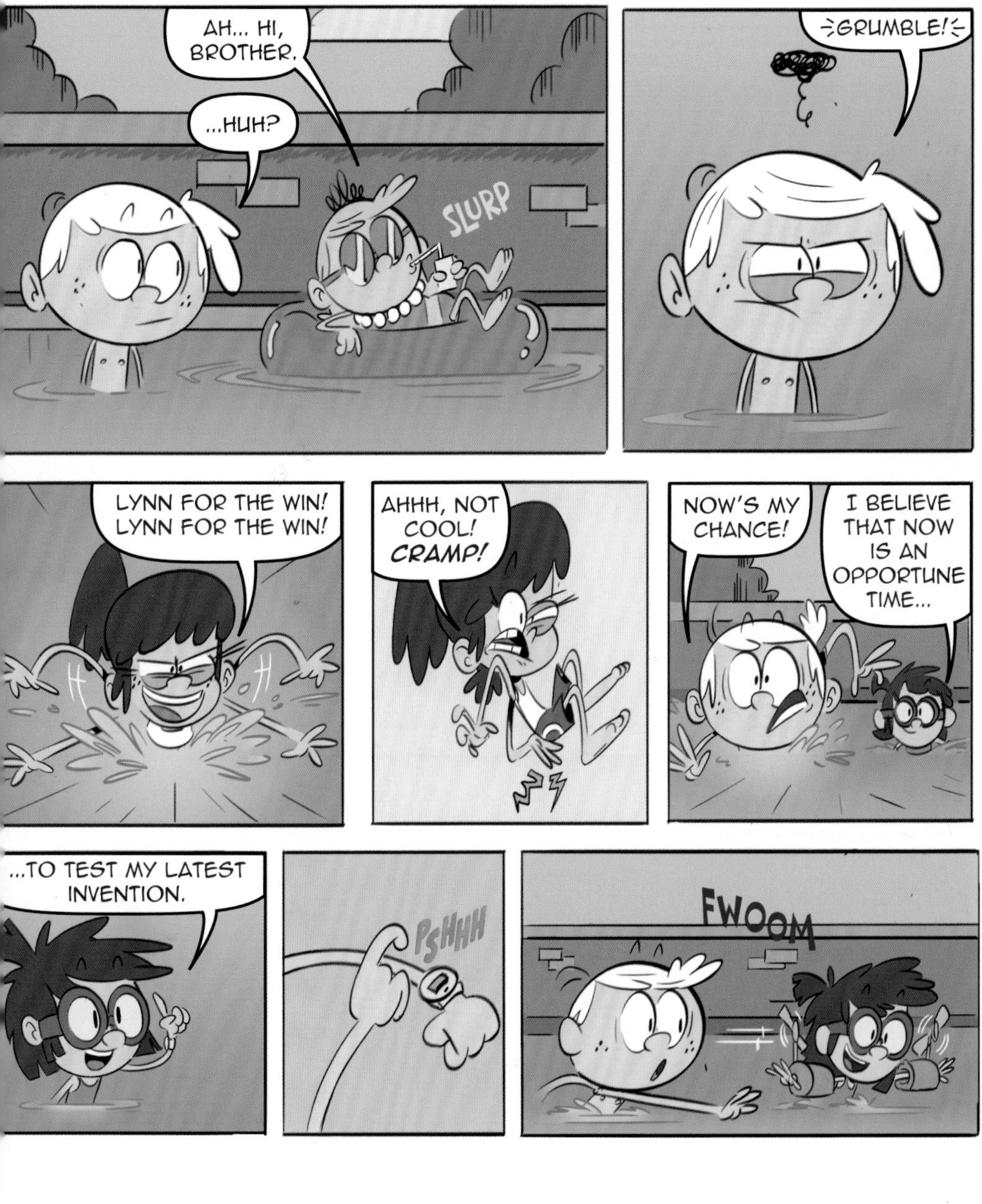
AH... HI, BROTHER.
...HUH?
SLURP
GRUMBLE!
LYNN FOR THE WIN! LYNN FOR THE WIN!
AHHH, NOT COOL! CRAMP!
NOW'S MY CHANCE!
I BELIEVE THAT NOW IS AN OPPORTUNE TIME...
...TO TEST MY LATEST INVENTION.
PSHHH
FWOOM

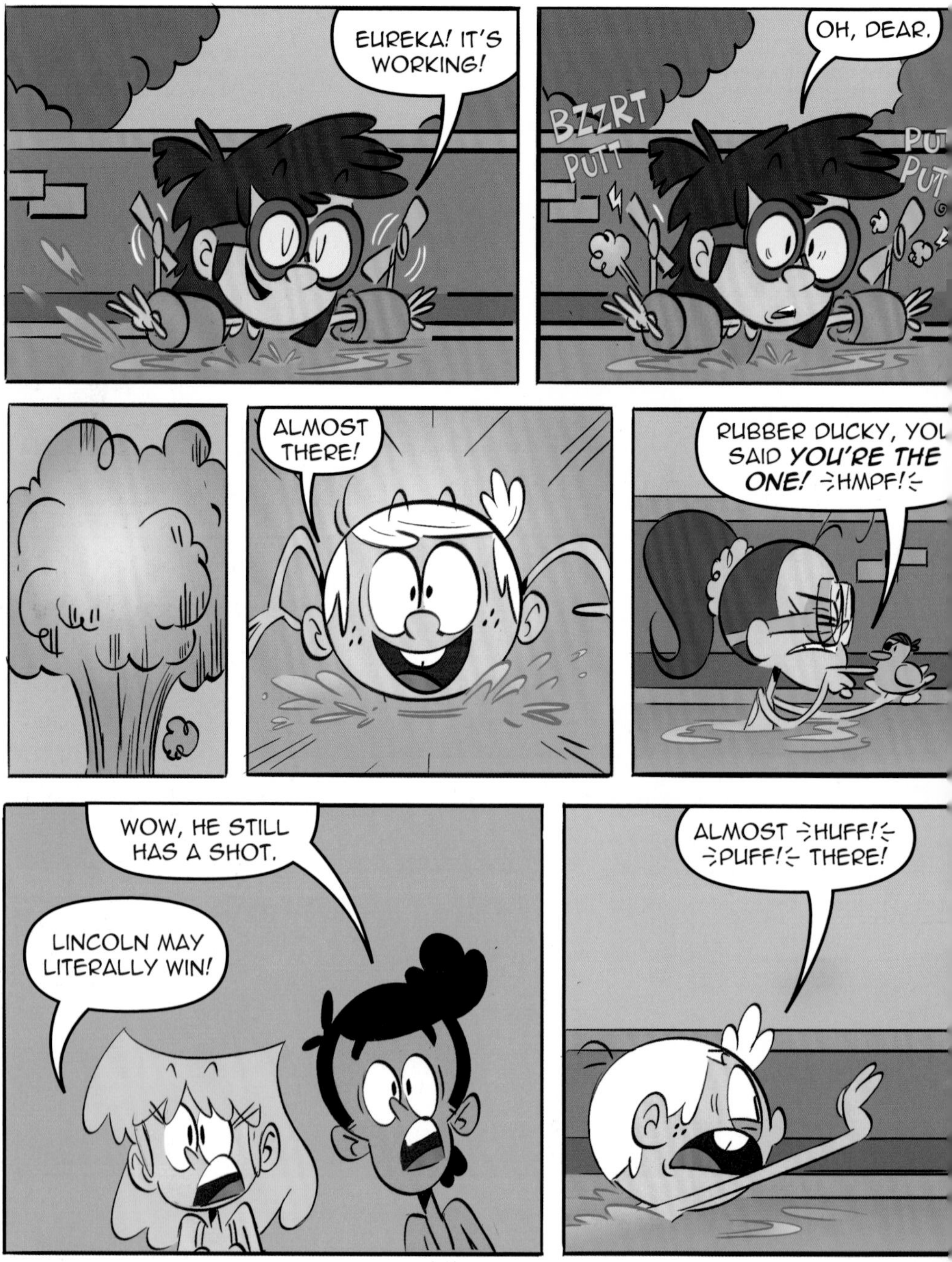
EUREKA! IT'S WORKING!
OH, DEAR.
BZZRT
PUTT
ALMOST THERE!
RUBBER DUCKY, YOU SAID YOU'RE THE ONE! HMPF!
WOW, HE STILL HAS A SHOT.
LINCOLN MAY LITERALLY WIN!
ALMOST HUFF! PUFF! THERE!

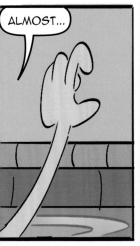

ALMOST...

HEAD FOR THE HILLS, SIBLINGS, POST HASTE!

SPITZ

SPUTTER

INSTEAD OF TREADING WATER, I AM RETAINING IT!

SLURP

I GOT NOTHING. THIS SUCKS THE FUN OUT OF IT, DOESN'T IT?

I DO FEEL A BIT MORE SHALLOW.

7 FT

5 FT

SLURP

I'M WINNING! IN YOUR *FACE*, LYNN!

DANG IT! WHERE'D THE WATER GO?

THUD

APOLOGIES, SIBLINGS, I SHOULD'VE MENTIONED THAT THESE WINGS HAVEN'T BEEN FIELD TESTED.

AWW, MAN, I WAS JUST ABOUT TO BEAT *STINKIN'*.

CAN SOMEBODY GET ME DOWN FROM HERE?

⋛GRR!⋚ SOMEBODY SPILLED MY JUICE!

JUICED WHEN THIS DAY COULDN'T GET ANY WORSE, HUH, SIS?

MY POOL! MY JOB!

MY CONDOLENCES, BOBBY. BUT YOU'RE TALL, DO YOU MIND HELPING ME GET DOWN?

⋛SIGH.⋚ GUESS IT'S TIME TO FIND A *NEW* SUMMER JOB...

THERE ARE LITERALLY PLENTY OF POOLS AROUND!

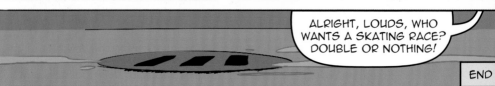

ALRIGHT, LOUDS, WHO WANTS A SKATING RACE? DOUBLE OR NOTHING!

END

"CUSTOMER APPRECIATION"

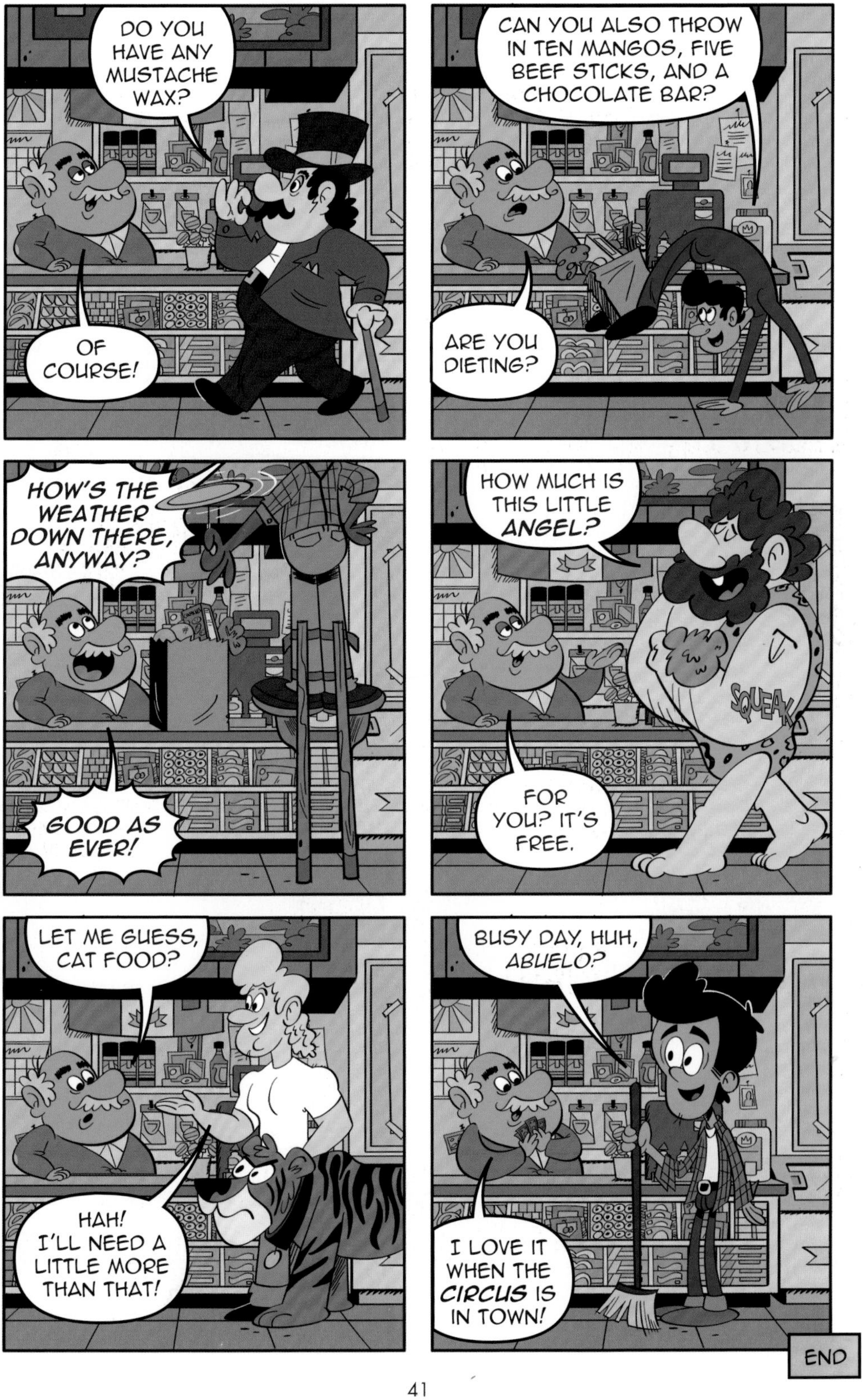
DO YOU HAVE ANY MUSTACHE WAX?
OF COURSE!
CAN YOU ALSO THROW IN TEN MANGOS, FIVE BEEF STICKS, AND A CHOCOLATE BAR?
ARE YOU DIETING?
HOW'S THE WEATHER DOWN THERE, ANYWAY?
GOOD AS EVER!
HOW MUCH IS THIS LITTLE ANGEL?
SQUEAK
FOR YOU? IT'S FREE.
LET ME GUESS, CAT FOOD?
HAH! I'LL NEED A LITTLE MORE THAN THAT!
BUSY DAY, HUH, ABUELO?
I LOVE IT WHEN THE CIRCUS IS IN TOWN!
END

"ROBOT RUMPUS"

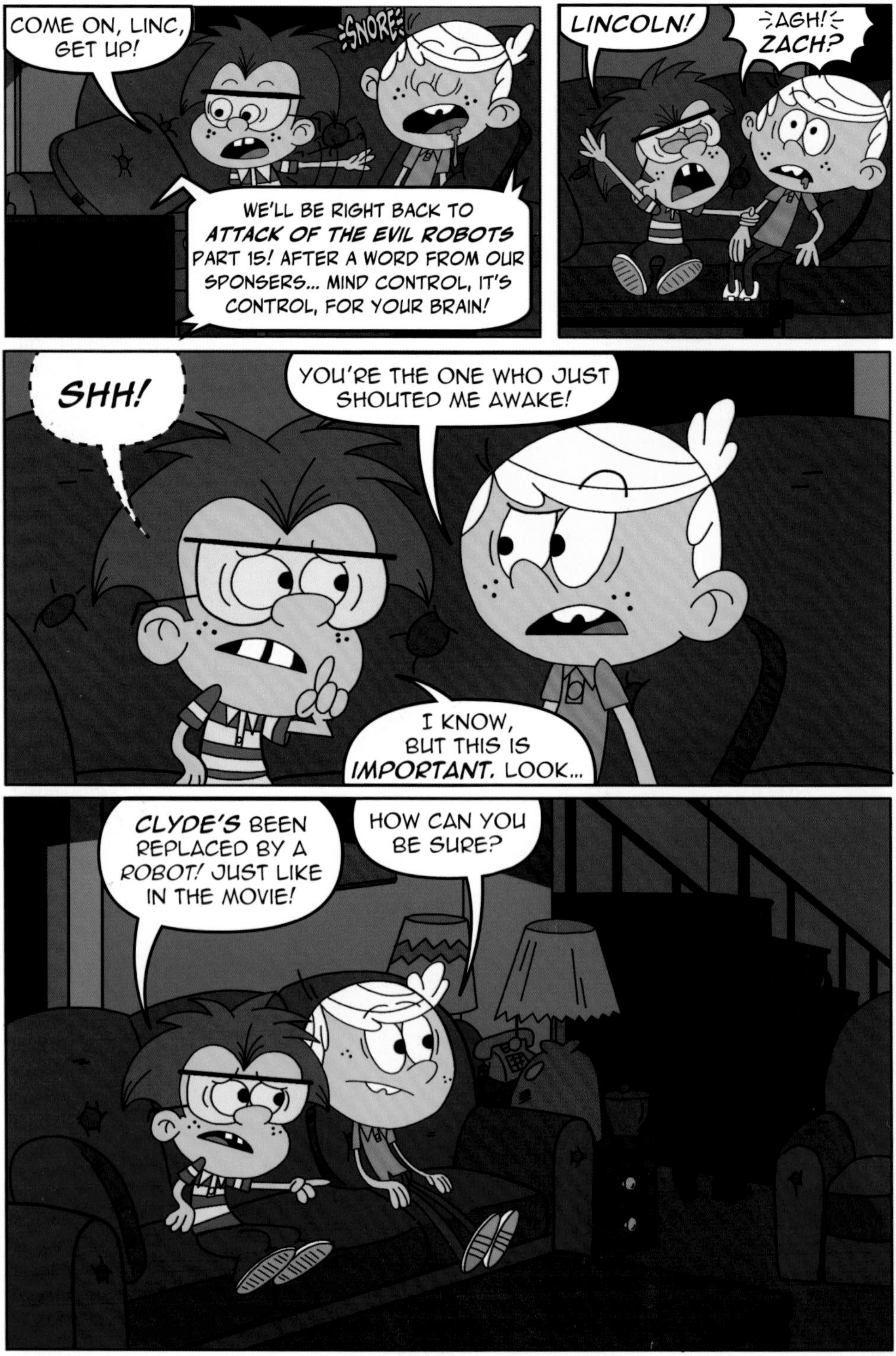

COME ON, LINC, GET UP!
SNORE
WE'LL BE RIGHT BACK TO ATTACK OF THE EVIL ROBOTS PART 15! AFTER A WORD FROM OUR SPONSERS... MIND CONTROL, IT'S CONTROL, FOR YOUR BRAIN!
LINCOLN!
AGH! ZACH?
SHH!
YOU'RE THE ONE WHO JUST SHOUTED ME AWAKE!
I KNOW, BUT THIS IS IMPORTANT. LOOK...
CLYDE'S BEEN REPLACED BY A ROBOT! JUST LIKE IN THE MOVIE!
HOW CAN YOU BE SURE?

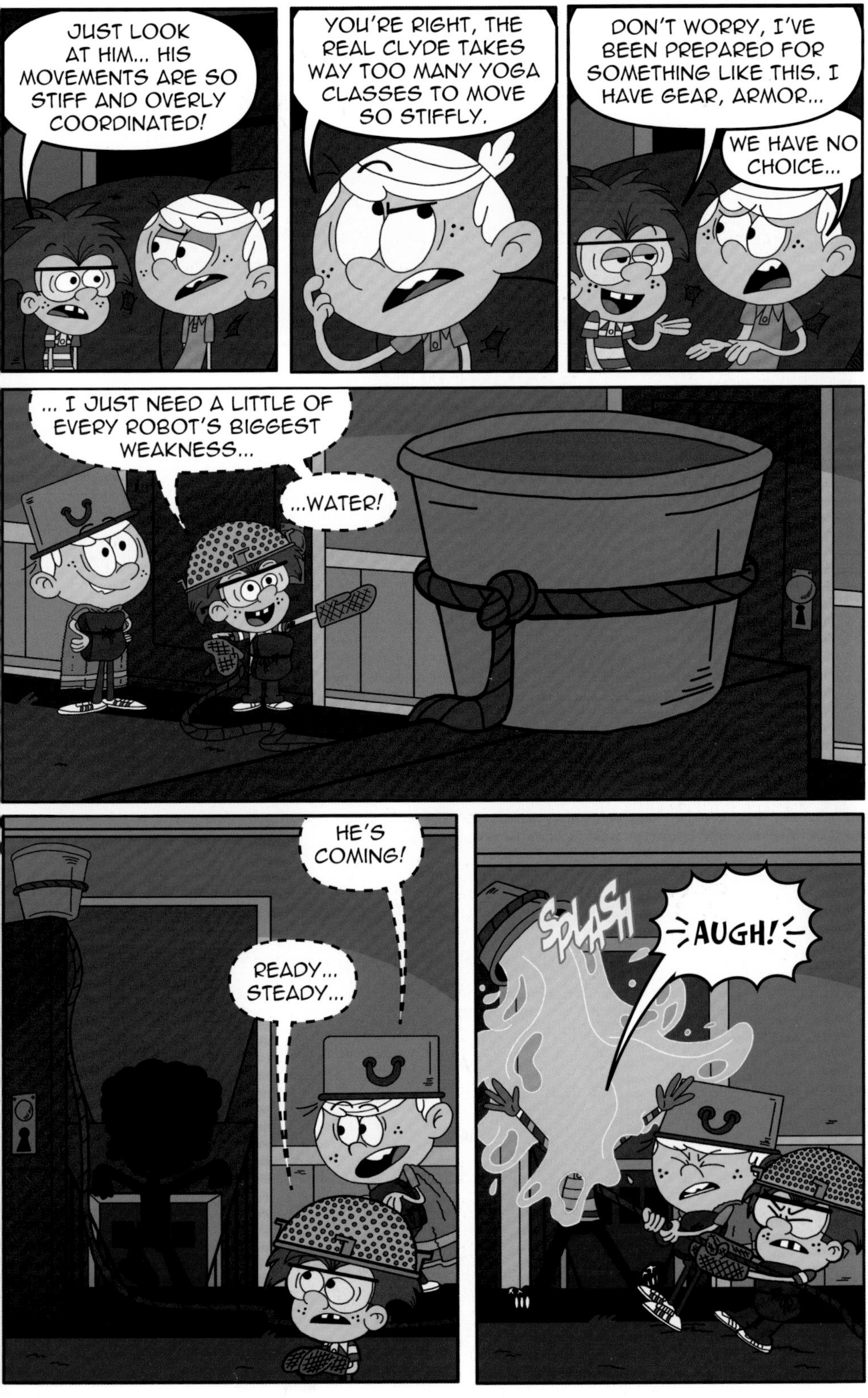
JUST LOOK AT HIM... HIS MOVEMENTS ARE SO STIFF AND OVERLY COORDINATED!
YOU'RE RIGHT, THE REAL CLYDE TAKES WAY TOO MANY YOGA CLASSES TO MOVE SO STIFFLY.
DON'T WORRY, I'VE BEEN PREPARED FOR SOMETHING LIKE THIS. I HAVE GEAR, ARMOR...
WE HAVE NO CHOICE...
... I JUST NEED A LITTLE OF EVERY ROBOT'S BIGGEST WEAKNESS...
...WATER!
HE'S COMING!
READY... STEADY...
SPLASH
AUGH!

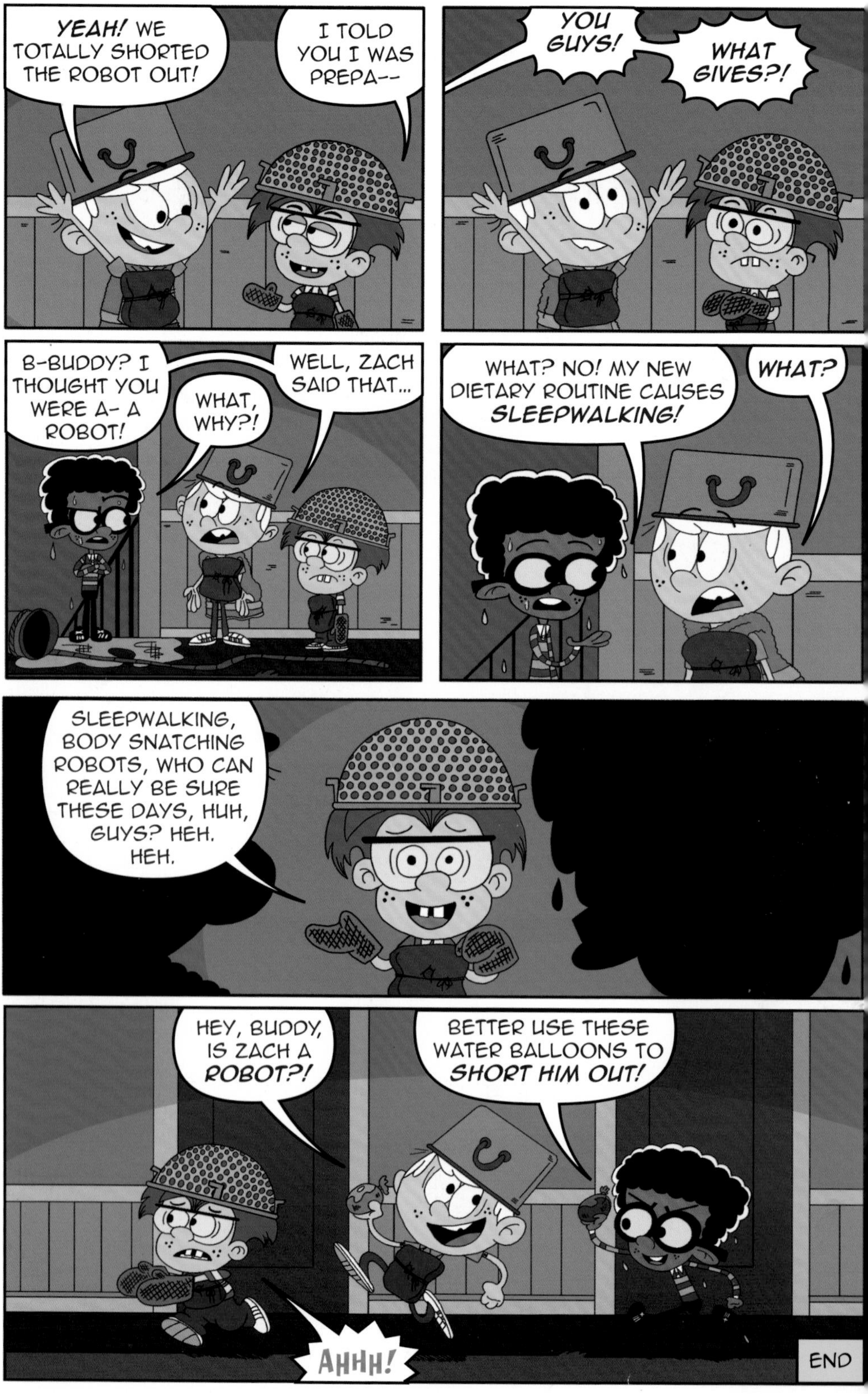
YEAH! WE TOTALLY SHORTED THE ROBOT OUT!
I TOLD YOU I WAS PREPA--
YOU GUYS!
WHAT GIVES?!
B-BUDDY? I THOUGHT YOU WERE A- A ROBOT!
WELL, ZACH SAID THAT...
WHAT, WHY?!
WHAT? NO! MY NEW DIETARY ROUTINE CAUSES SLEEPWALKING!
WHAT?
SLEEPWALKING, BODY SNATCHING ROBOTS, WHO CAN REALLY BE SURE THESE DAYS, HUH, GUYS? HEH. HEH.
HEY, BUDDY, IS ZACH A ROBOT?!
BETTER USE THESE WATER BALLOONS TO SHORT HIM OUT!
AHHH!
END

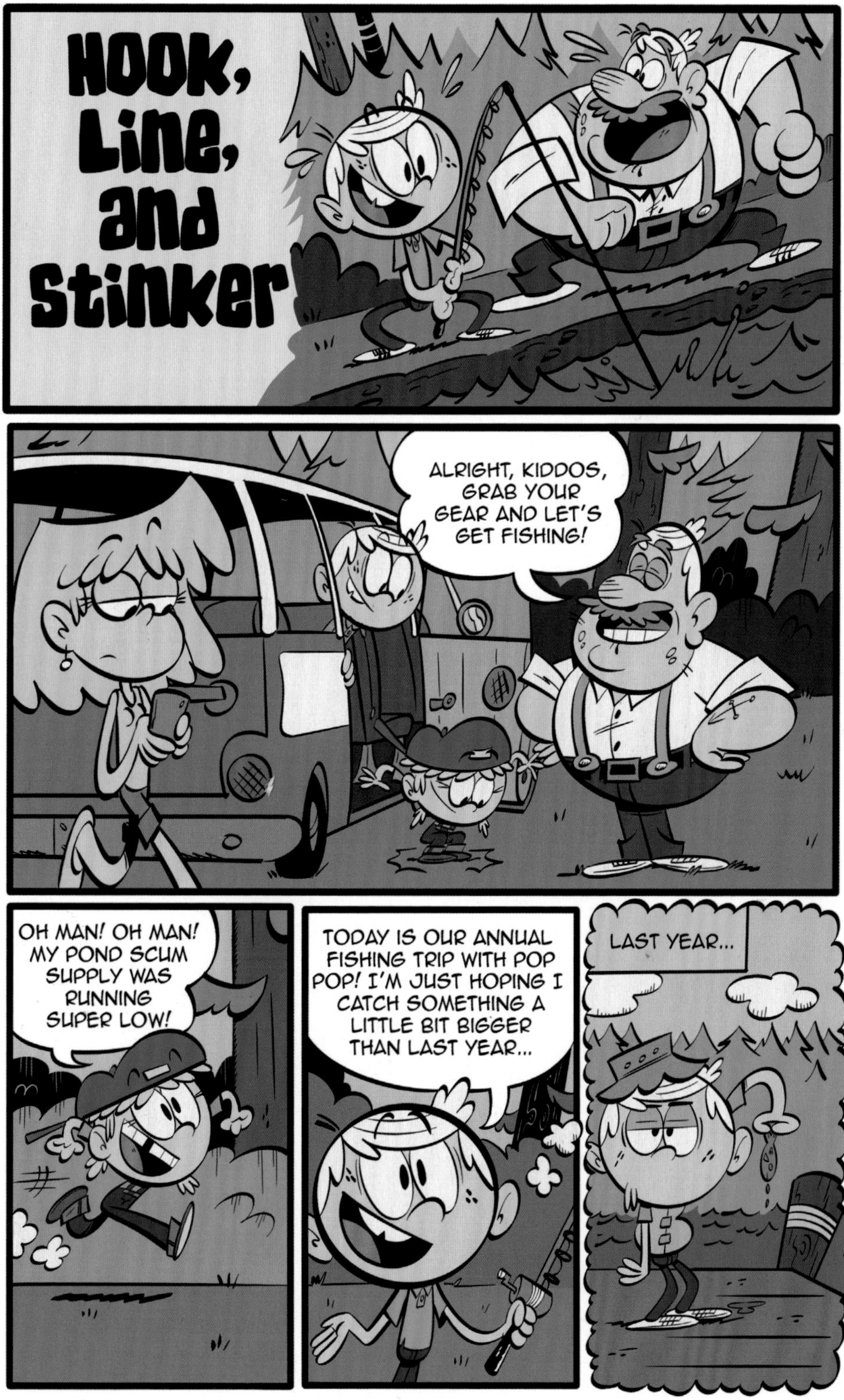
HOOK, Line, and Stinker
ALRIGHT, KIDDOS, GRAB YOUR GEAR AND LET'S GET FISHING!
OH MAN! OH MAN! MY POND SCUM SUPPLY WAS RUNNING SUPER LOW!
TODAY IS OUR ANNUAL FISHING TRIP WITH POP POP! I'M JUST HOPING I CATCH SOMETHING A LITTLE BIT BIGGER THAN LAST YEAR...
LAST YEAR...

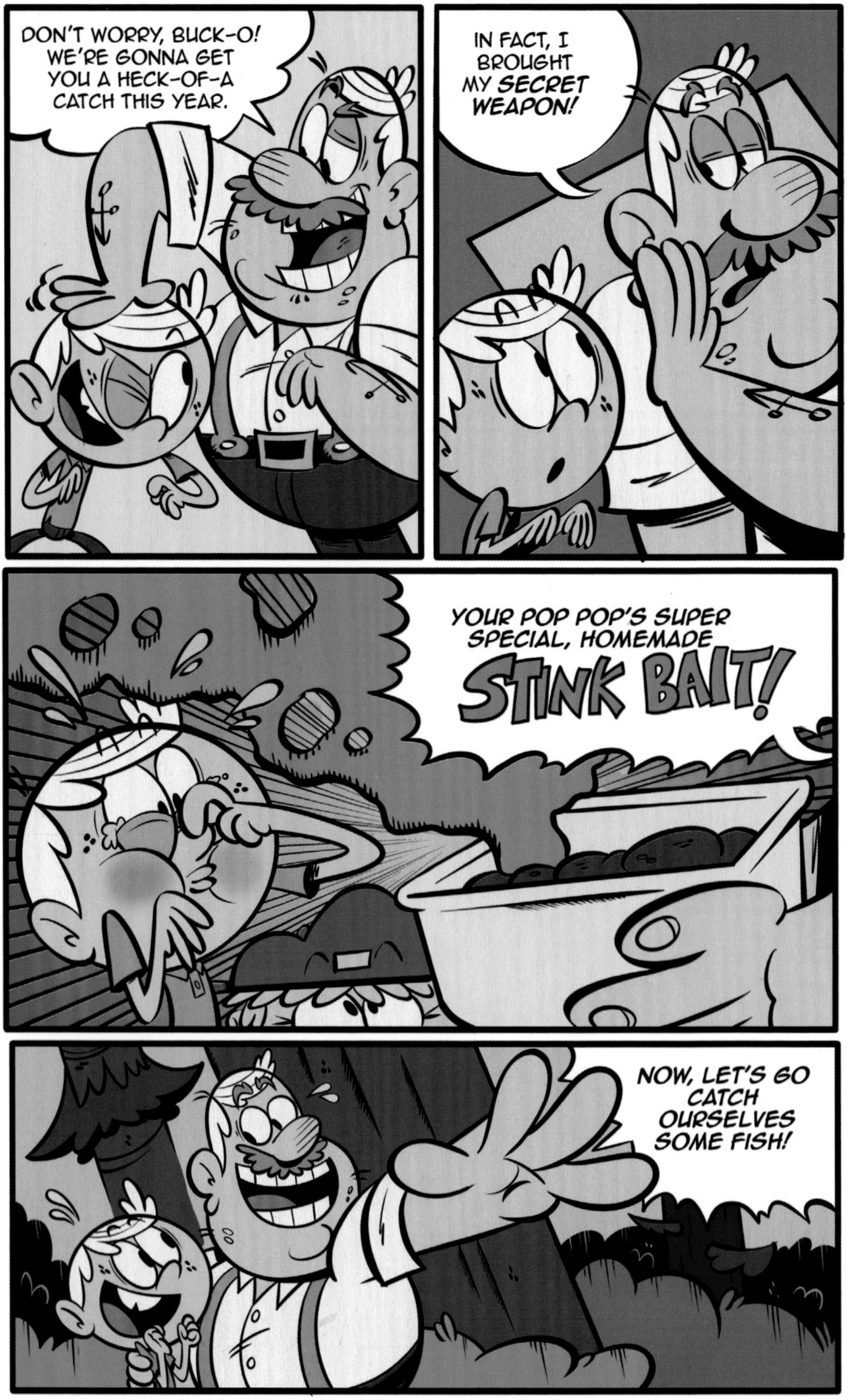
DON'T WORRY, BUCK-O! WE'RE GONNA GET YOU A HECK-OF-A CATCH THIS YEAR.
IN FACT, I BROUGHT MY SECRET WEAPON!
YOUR POP POP'S SUPER SPECIAL, HOMEMADE
STINK BAIT!
NOW, LET'S GO CATCH OURSELVES SOME FISH!

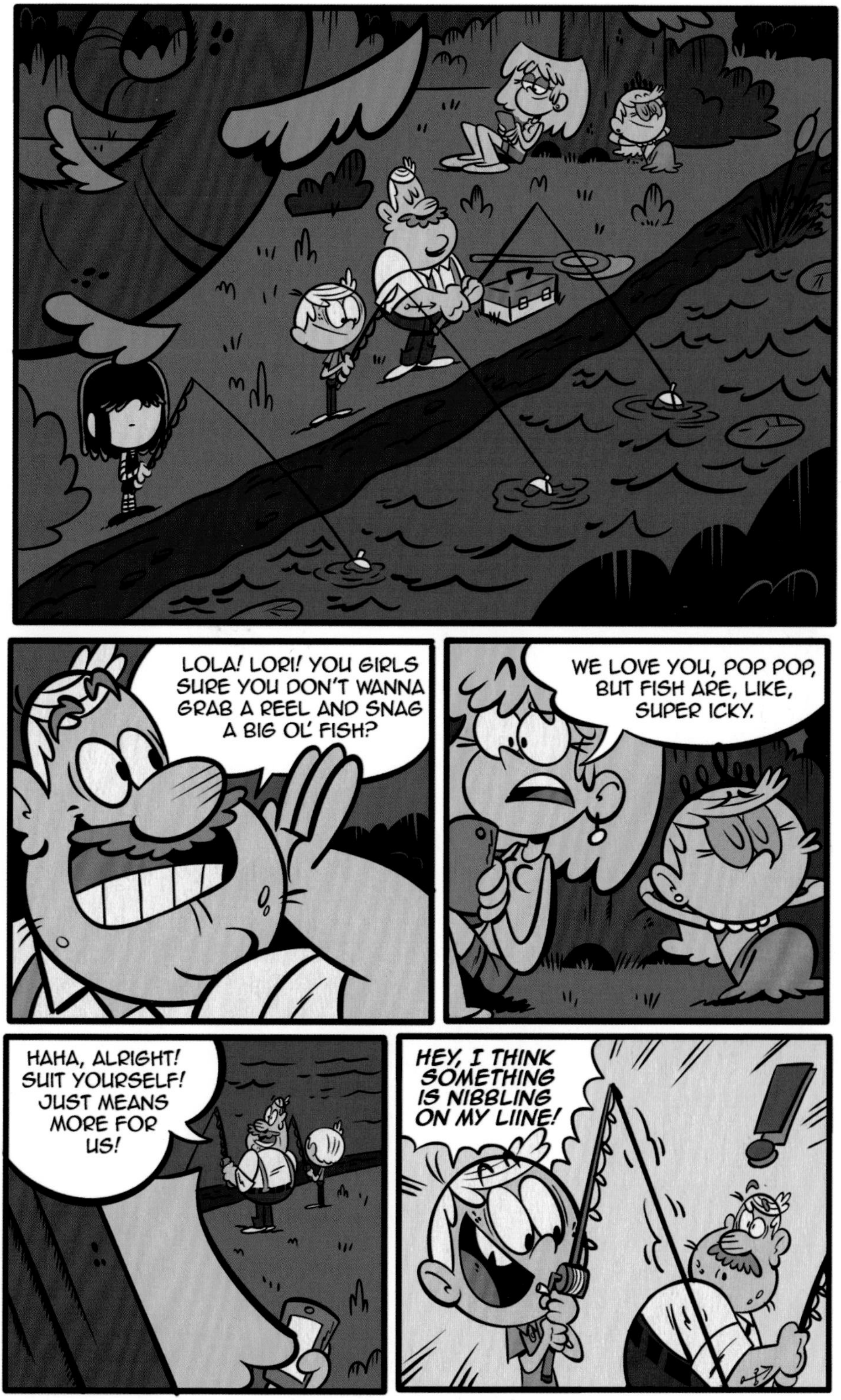
LOLA! LORI! YOU GIRLS SURE YOU DON'T WANNA GRAB A REEL AND SNAG A BIG OL' FISH?
WE LOVE YOU, POP POP, BUT FISH ARE, LIKE, SUPER ICKY.
HAHA, ALRIGHT! SUIT YOURSELF! JUST MEANS MORE FOR US!
HEY, I THINK SOMETHING IS NIBBLING ON MY LIINE!
!

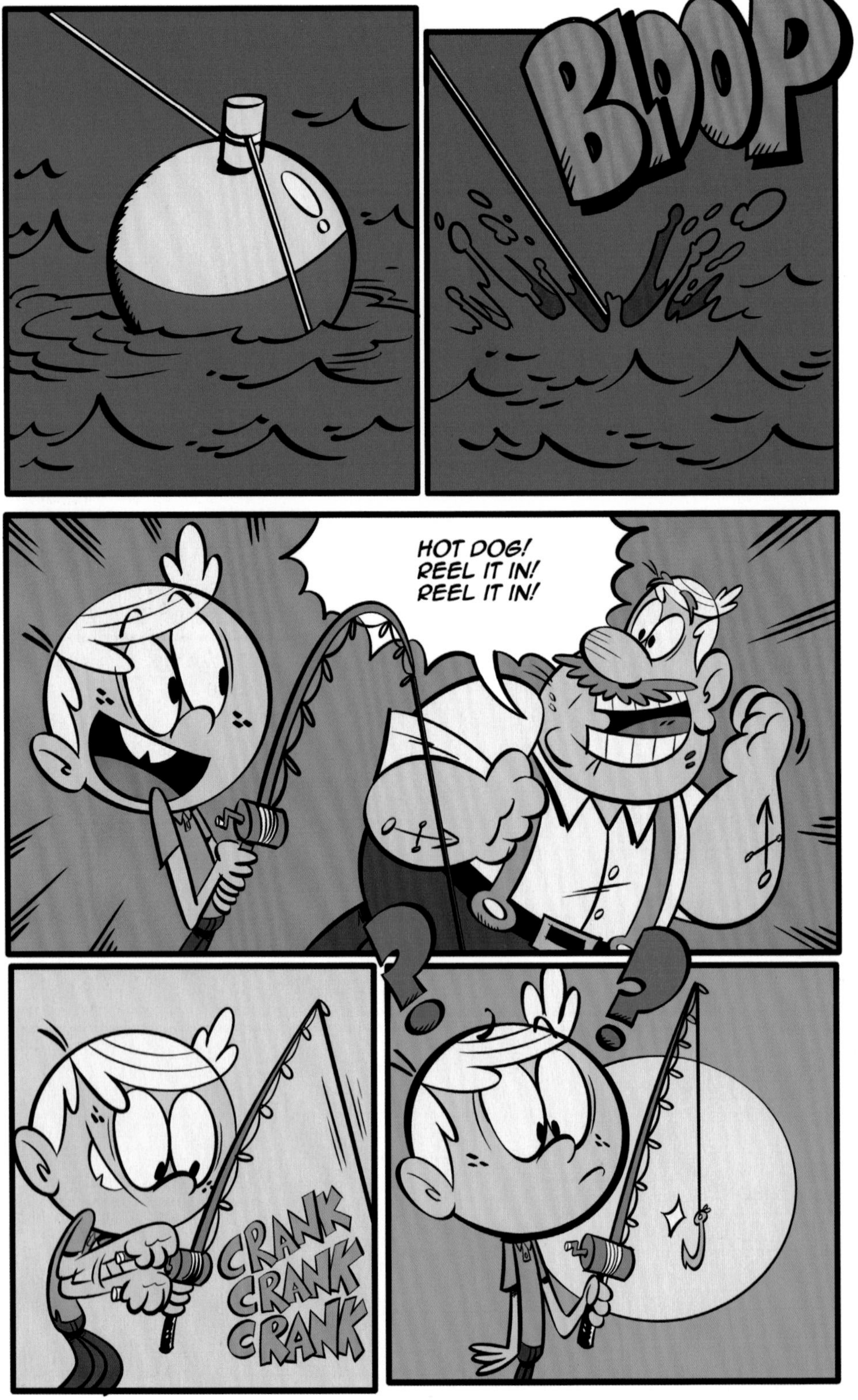
BLOOP
HOT DOG!
REEL IT IN!
REEL IT IN!
CRANK
CRANK
CRANK

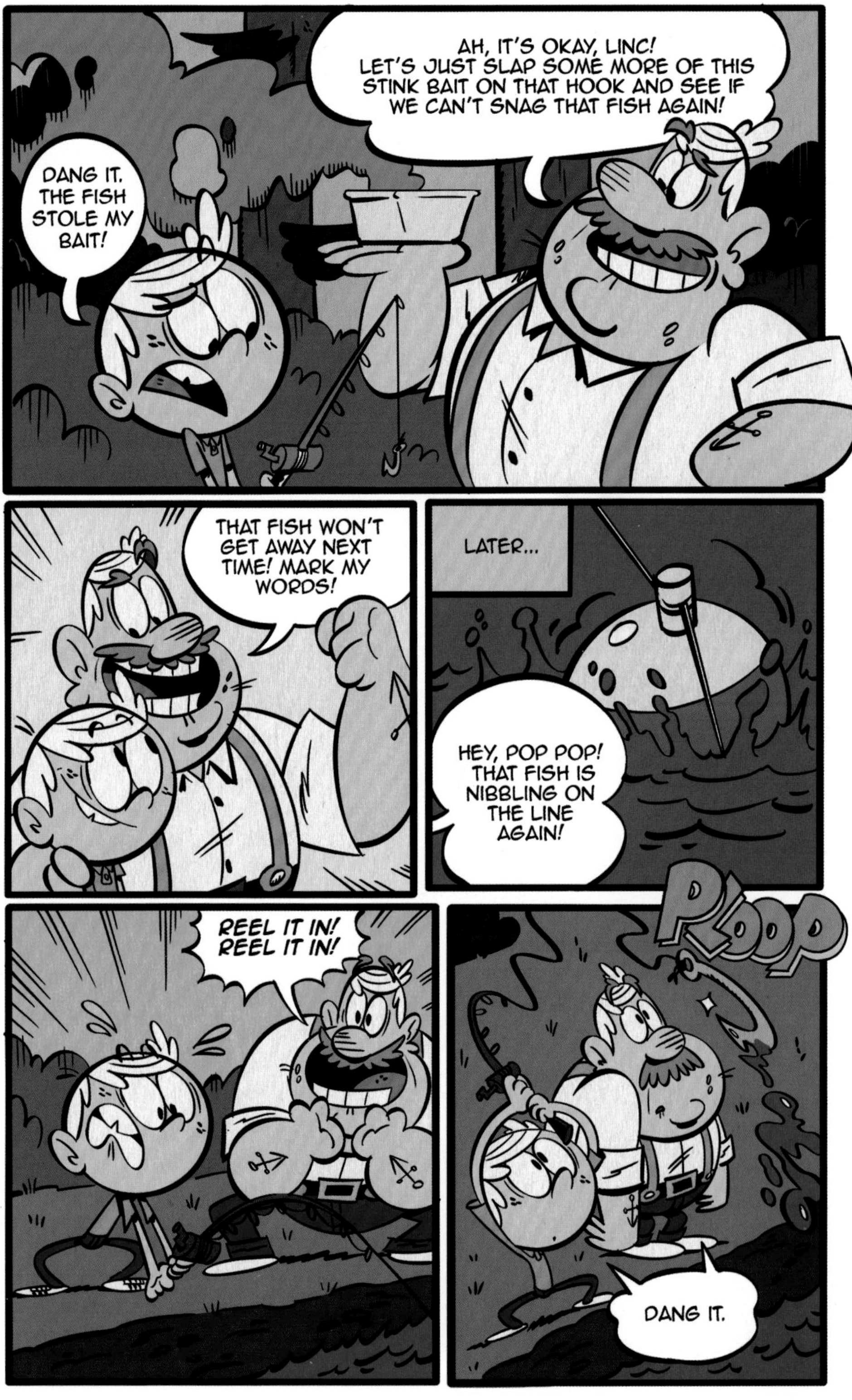
AH, IT'S OKAY, LINC! LET'S JUST SLAP SOME MORE OF THIS STINK BAIT ON THAT HOOK AND SEE IF WE CAN'T SNAG THAT FISH AGAIN!
DANG IT. THE FISH STOLE MY BAIT!
THAT FISH WON'T GET AWAY NEXT TIME! MARK MY WORDS!
LATER...
HEY, POP POP! THAT FISH IS NIBBLING ON THE LINE AGAIN!
REEL IT IN! REEL IT IN!
PLOOP
DANG IT.

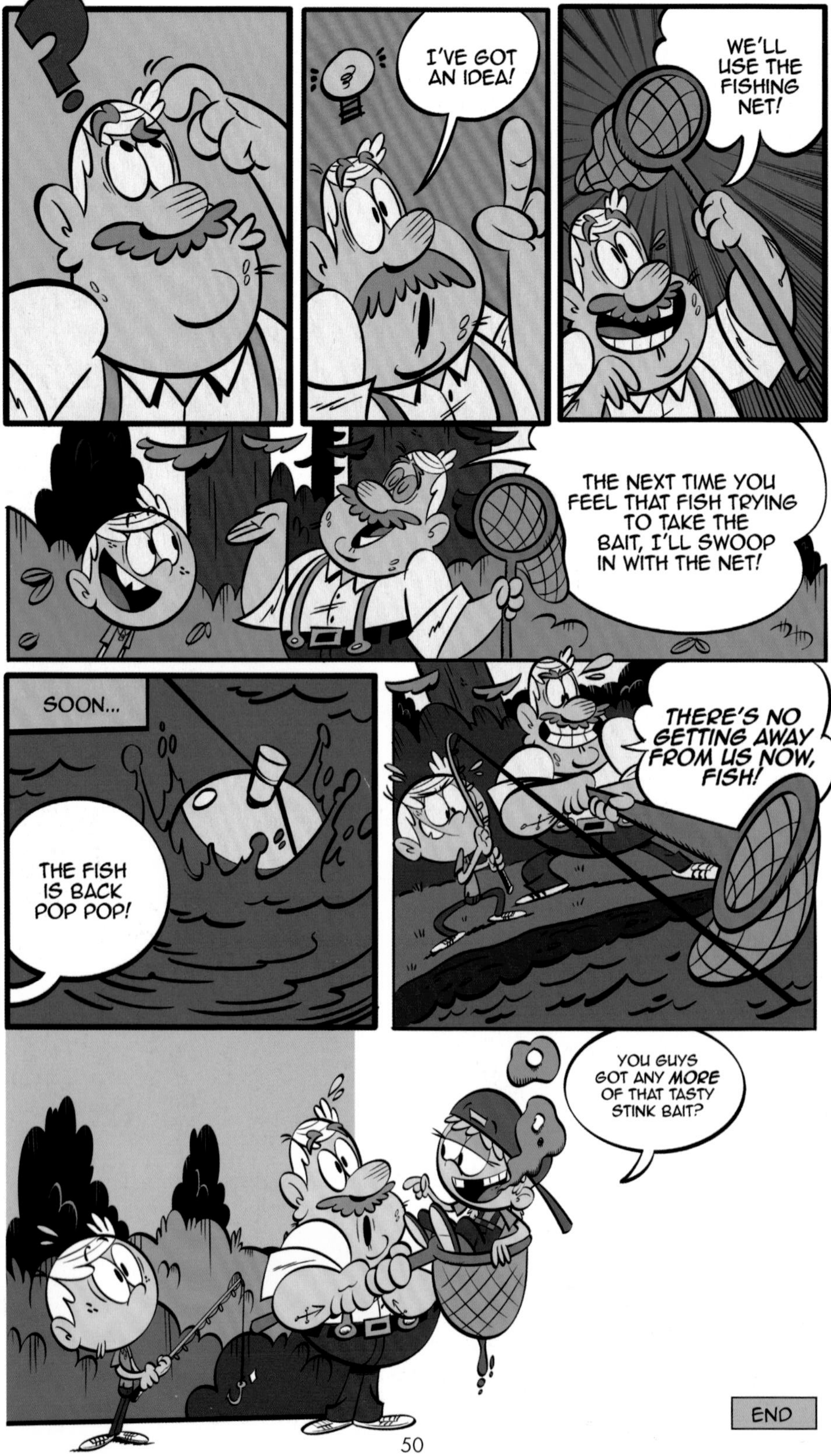
?
I'VE GOT AN IDEA!
WE'LL USE THE FISHING NET!
THE NEXT TIME YOU FEEL THAT FISH TRYING TO TAKE THE BAIT, I'LL SWOOP IN WITH THE NET!
SOON...
THE FISH IS BACK POP POP!
THERE'S NO GETTING AWAY FROM US NOW, FISH!
YOU GUYS GOT ANY MORE OF THAT TASTY STINK BAIT?
END

"ONE, TWO, SWITCHEROO"

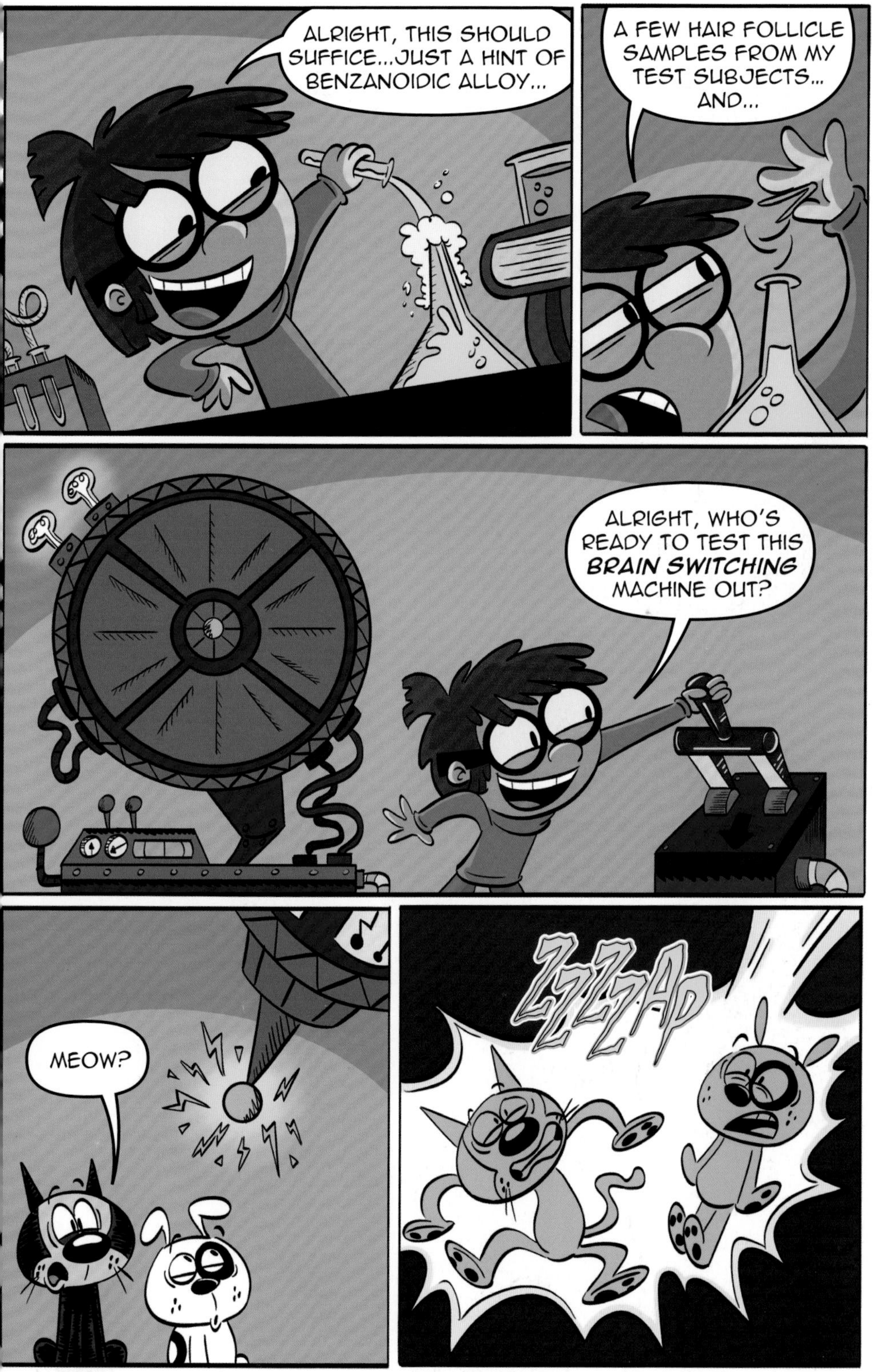
ALRIGHT, THIS SHOULD SUFFICE...JUST A HINT OF BENZANOIDIC ALLOY...
A FEW HAIR FOLLICLE SAMPLES FROM MY TEST SUBJECTS... AND...
ALRIGHT, WHO'S READY TO TEST THIS BRAIN SWITCHING MACHINE OUT?
MEOW?
ZZZZAP

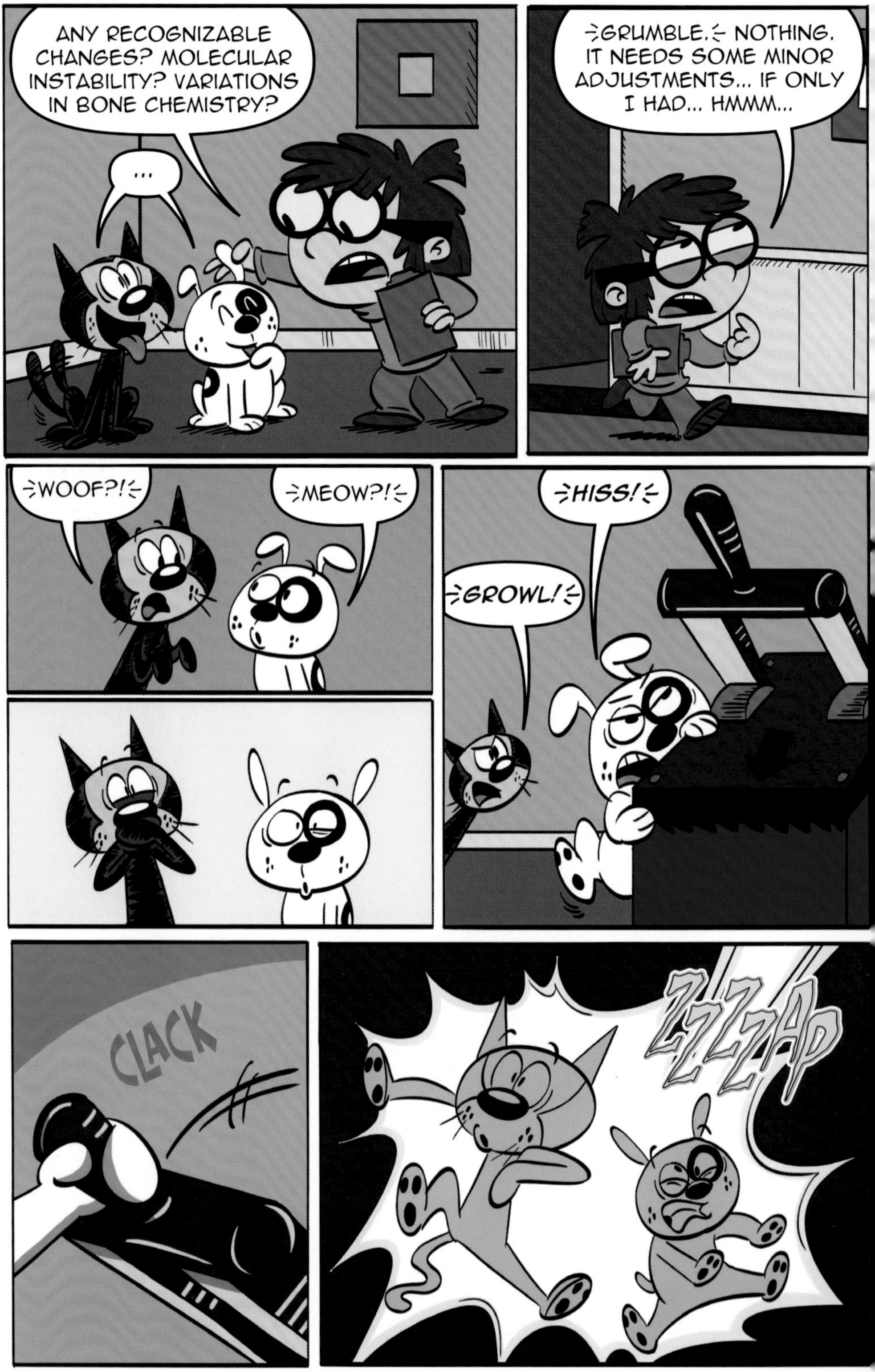
ANY RECOGNIZABLE CHANGES? MOLECULAR INSTABILITY? VARIATIONS IN BONE CHEMISTRY?
...
GRUMBLE. NOTHING. IT NEEDS SOME MINOR ADJUSTMENTS... IF ONLY I HAD... HMMM...
WOOF?!
MEOW?!
HISS!
GROWL!
CLACK
ZZZZAP

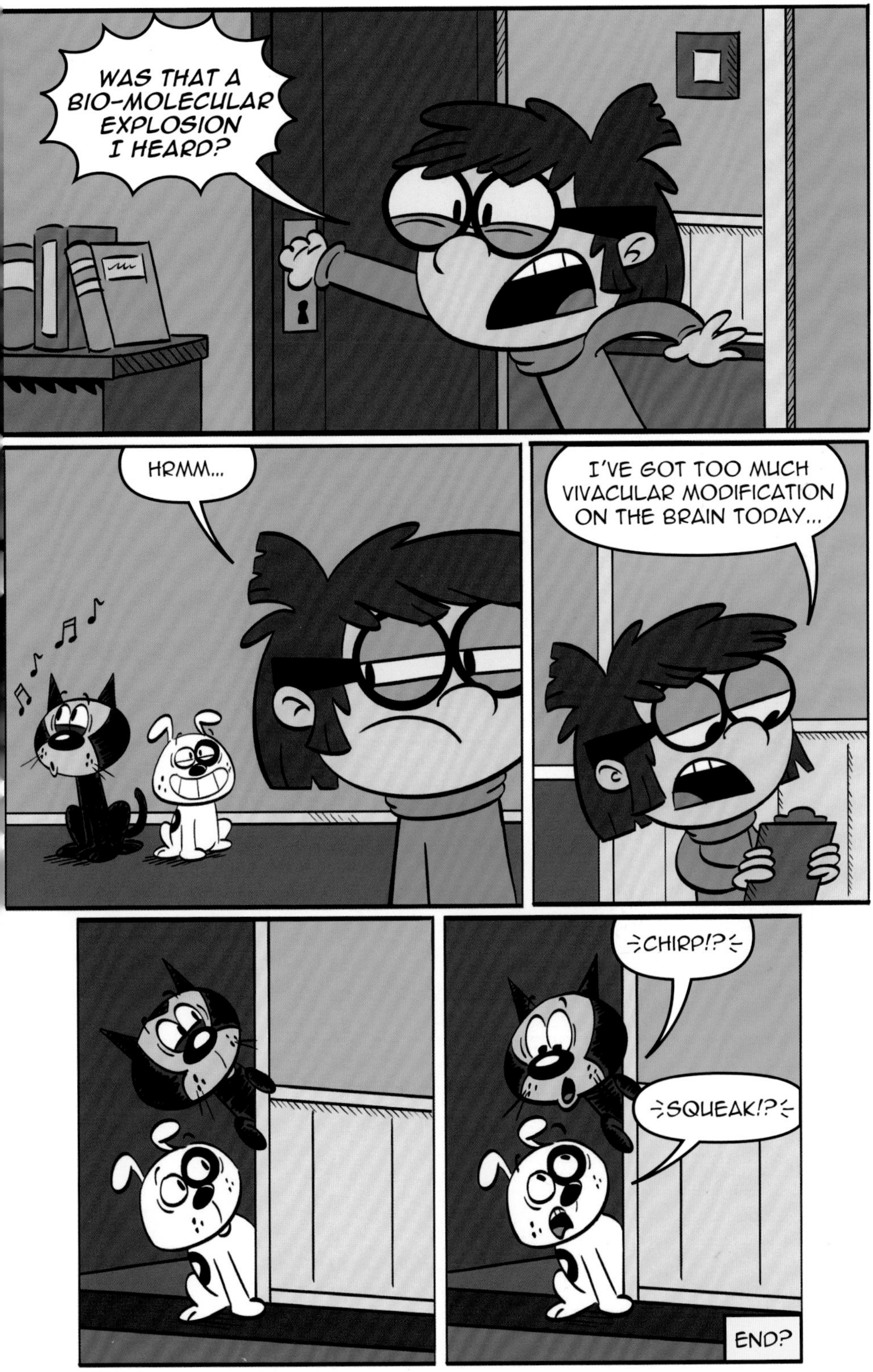
WAS THAT A BIO-MOLECULAR EXPLOSION I HEARD?
HRMM...
I'VE GOT TOO MUCH VIVACULAR MODIFICATION ON THE BRAIN TODAY...
CHIRP!?
SQUEAK!?
END?

"WHO'S THE LOUDEST?"

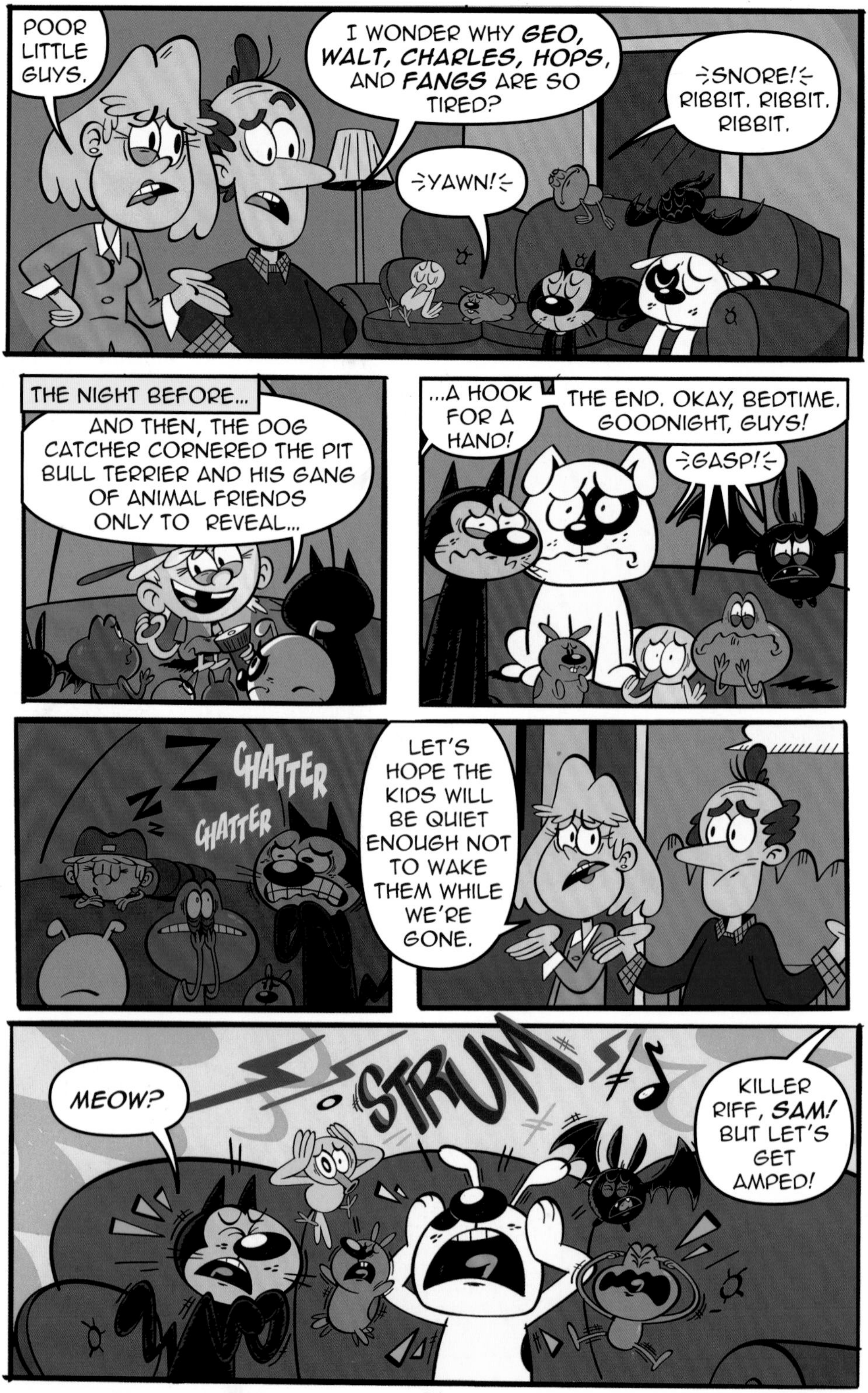
POOR LITTLE GUYS.
I WONDER WHY GEO, WALT, CHARLES, HOPS, AND FANGS ARE SO TIRED?
SNORE! RIBBIT. RIBBIT. RIBBIT.
YAWN!
THE NIGHT BEFORE...
AND THEN, THE DOG CATCHER CORNERED THE PIT BULL TERRIER AND HIS GANG OF ANIMAL FRIENDS ONLY TO REVEAL...
...A HOOK FOR A HAND!
THE END. OKAY, BEDTIME. GOODNIGHT, GUYS!
GASP!
Z Z Z
CHATTER
CHATTER
LET'S HOPE THE KIDS WILL BE QUIET ENOUGH NOT TO WAKE THEM WHILE WE'RE GONE.
MEOW?
STRUM
KILLER RIFF, SAM! BUT LET'S GET AMPED!

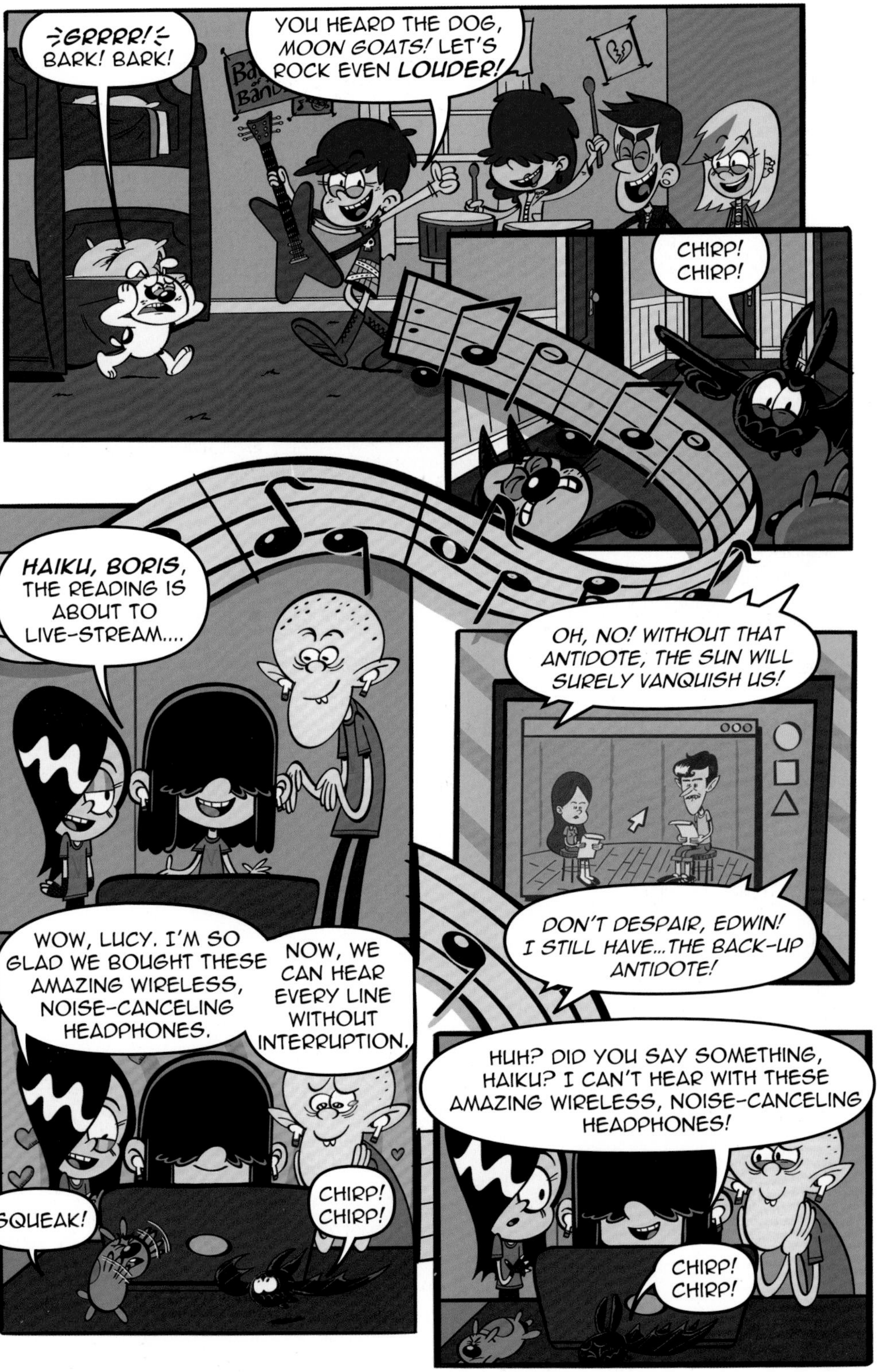

GRRRR! BARK! BARK!
YOU HEARD THE DOG, MOON GOATS! LET'S ROCK EVEN LOUDER!
CHIRP! CHIRP!
HAIKU, BORIS, THE READING IS ABOUT TO LIVE-STREAM....
OH, NO! WITHOUT THAT ANTIDOTE, THE SUN WILL SURELY VANQUISH US!
DON'T DESPAIR, EDWIN! I STILL HAVE...THE BACK-UP ANTIDOTE!
WOW, LUCY. I'M SO GLAD WE BOUGHT THESE AMAZING WIRELESS, NOISE-CANCELING HEADPHONES.
NOW, WE CAN HEAR EVERY LINE WITHOUT INTERRUPTION.
SQUEAK!
CHIRP! CHIRP!
HUH? DID YOU SAY SOMETHING, HAIKU? I CAN'T HEAR WITH THESE AMAZING WIRELESS, NOISE-CANCELING HEADPHONES!
CHIRP! CHIRP!

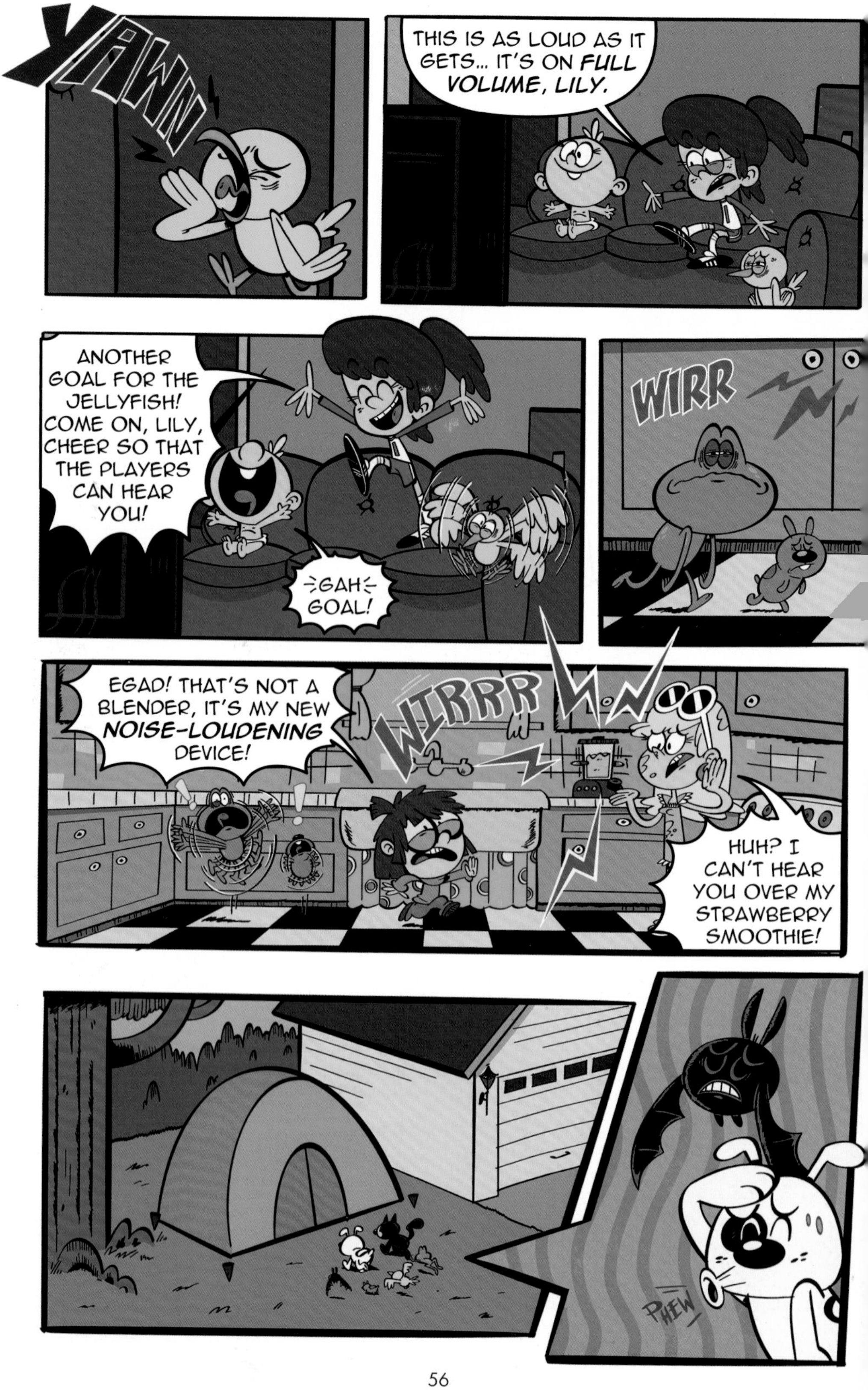
YAWN
THIS IS AS LOUD AS IT GETS... IT'S ON FULL VOLUME, LILY.
ANOTHER GOAL FOR THE JELLYFISH! COME ON, LILY, CHEER SO THAT THE PLAYERS CAN HEAR YOU!
GAH GOAL!
WIRR
EGAD! THAT'S NOT A BLENDER, IT'S MY NEW NOISE-LOUDENING DEVICE!
WIRRR
HUH? I CAN'T HEAR YOU OVER MY STRAWBERRY SMOOTHIE!
PHEW

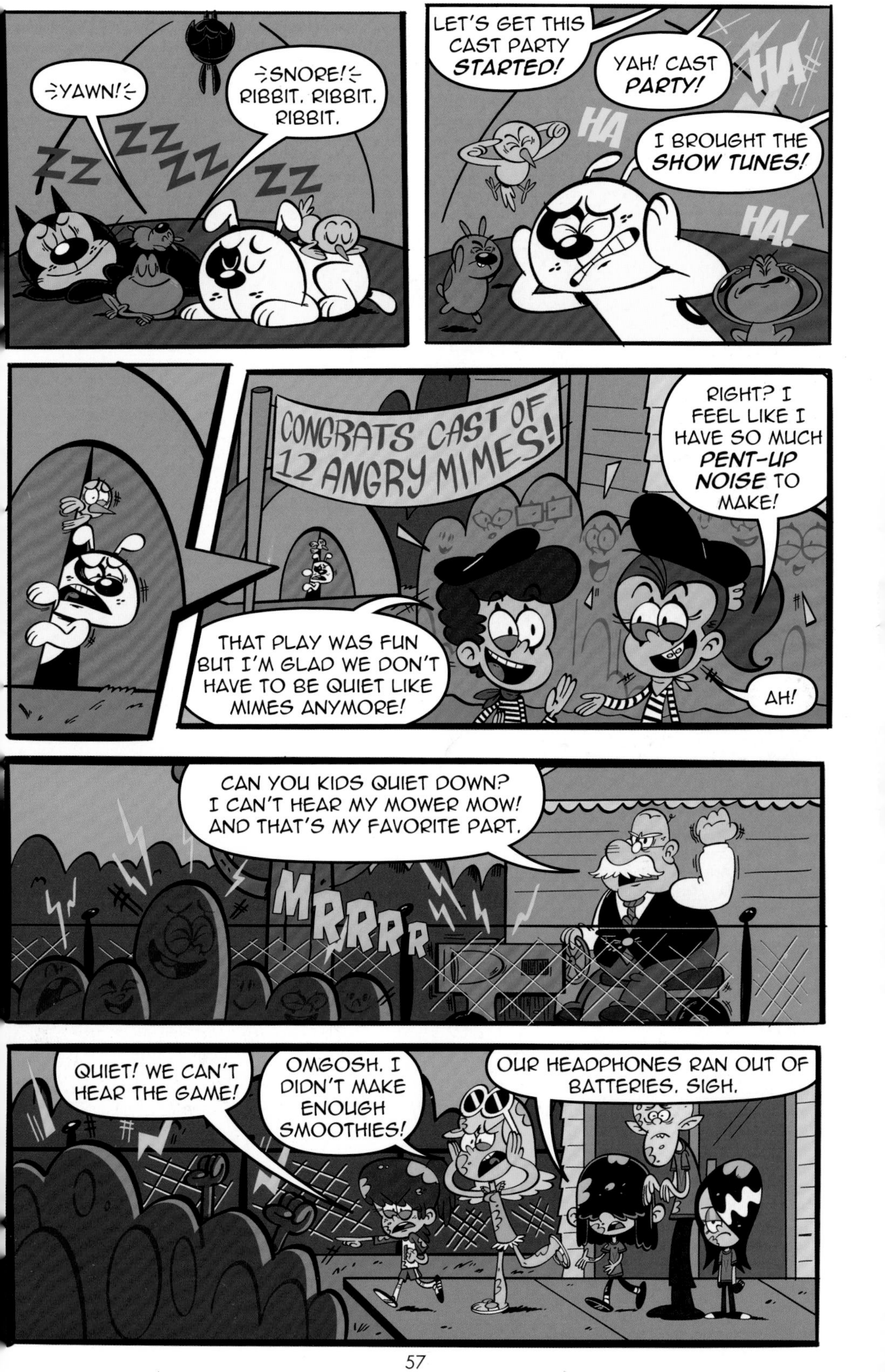

YAWN!
SNORE! RIBBIT. RIBBIT. RIBBIT.
ZZ ZZ ZZ ZZ
LET'S GET THIS CAST PARTY STARTED!
YAH! CAST PARTY!
HA HA HA HA!
I BROUGHT THE SHOW TUNES!
CONGRATS CAST OF 12 ANGRY MIMES!
THAT PLAY WAS FUN BUT I'M GLAD WE DON'T HAVE TO BE QUIET LIKE MIMES ANYMORE!
RIGHT? I FEEL LIKE I HAVE SO MUCH PENT-UP NOISE TO MAKE!
AH!
CAN YOU KIDS QUIET DOWN? I CAN'T HEAR MY MOWER MOW! AND THAT'S MY FAVORITE PART.
MRRRRR
QUIET! WE CAN'T HEAR THE GAME!
OMGOSH. I DIDN'T MAKE ENOUGH SMOOTHIES!
OUR HEADPHONES RAN OUT OF BATTERIES. SIGH.

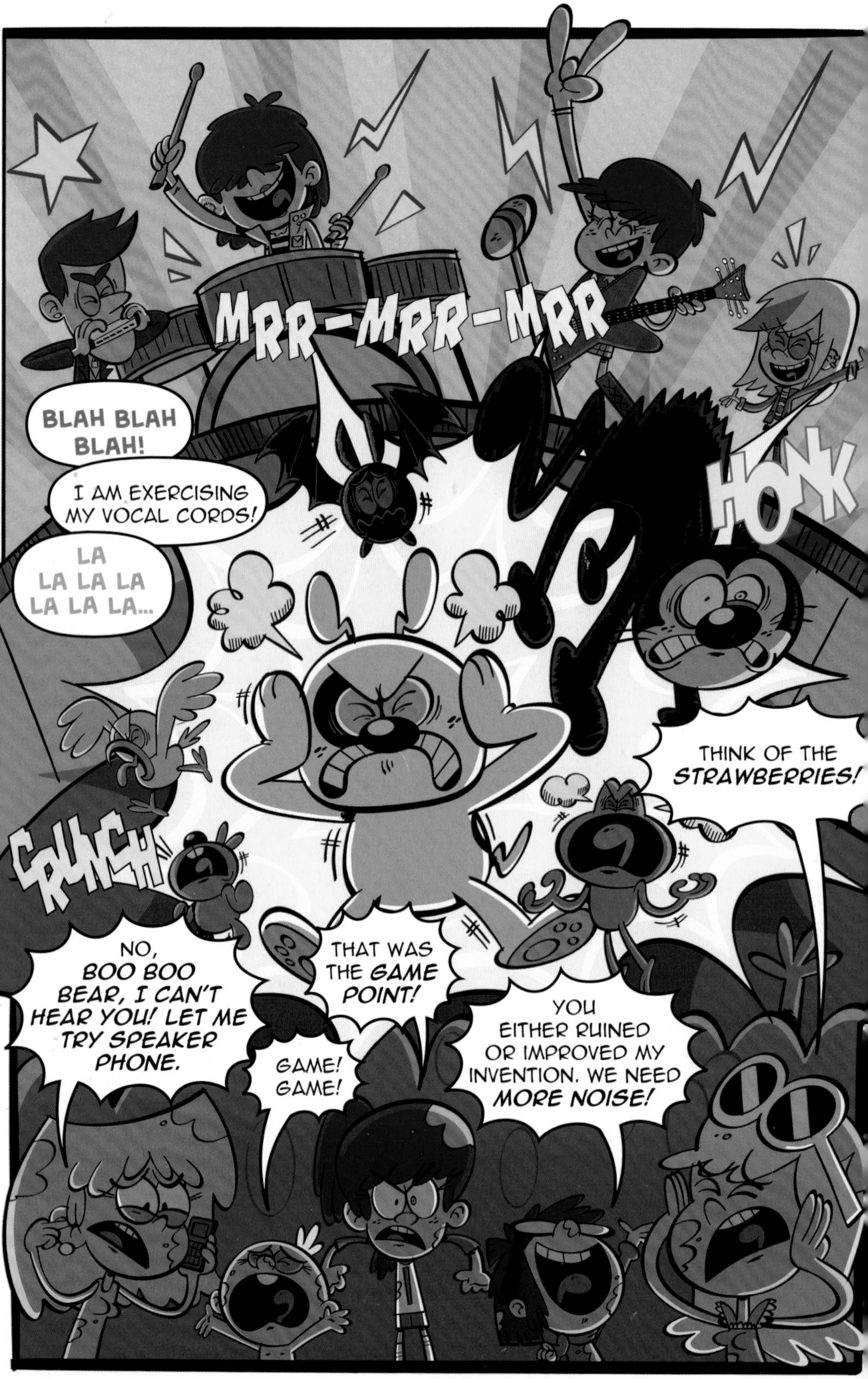
MRR-MRR-MRR
BLAH BLAH BLAH!
I AM EXERCISING MY VOCAL CORDS!
LA LA LA LA LA LA LA...
HONK
THINK OF THE STRAWBERRIES!
CRUNCH
NO, BOO BOO BEAR, I CAN'T HEAR YOU! LET ME TRY SPEAKER PHONE.
THAT WAS THE GAME POINT!
GAME! GAME!
YOU EITHER RUINED OR IMPROVED MY INVENTION. WE NEED MORE NOISE!

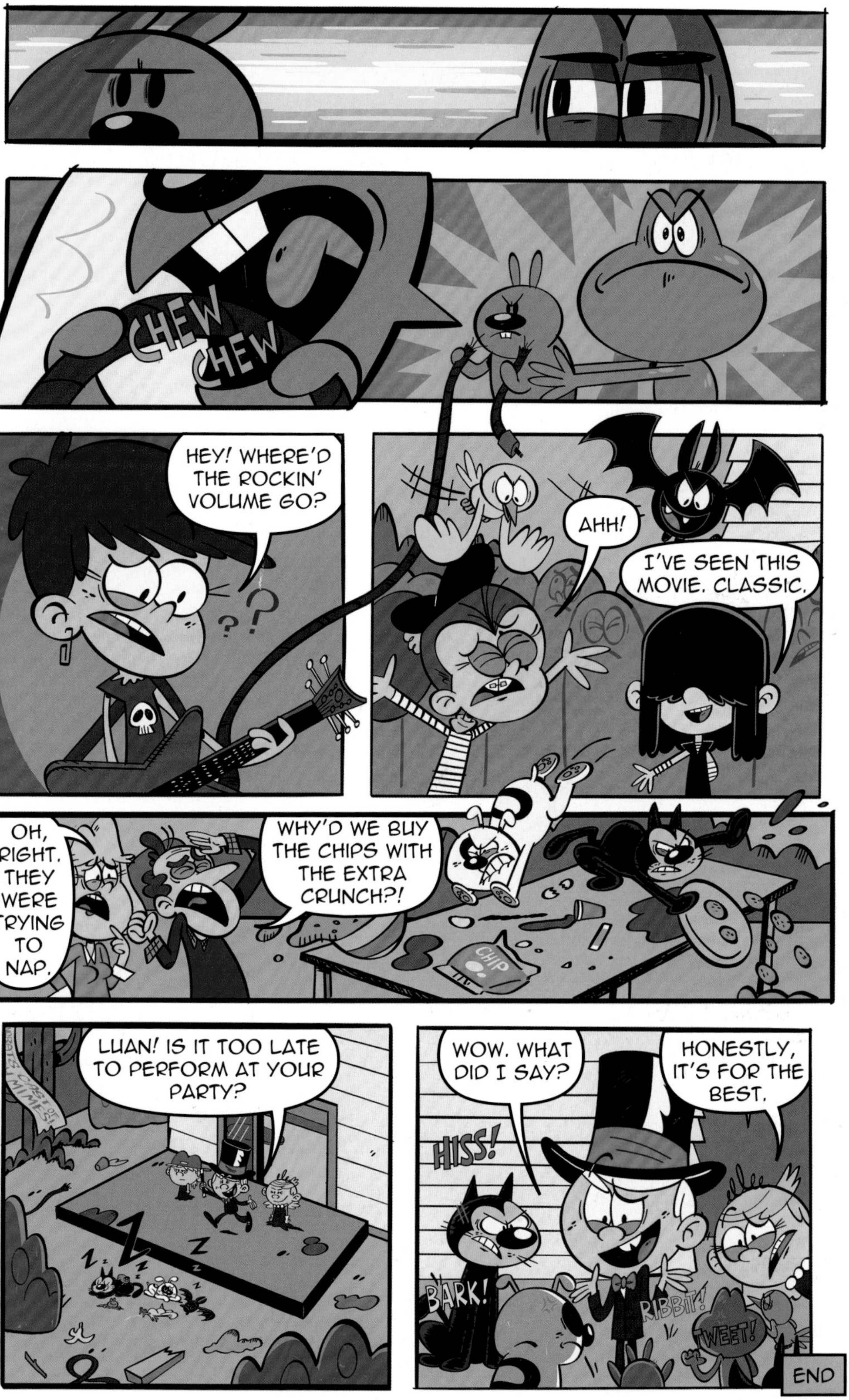
CHEW
CHEW
HEY! WHERE'D THE ROCKIN' VOLUME GO?
AHH!
I'VE SEEN THIS MOVIE. CLASSIC.
OH, RIGHT. THEY WERE TRYING TO NAP.
WHY'D WE BUY THE CHIPS WITH THE EXTRA CRUNCH?!
CHIP
LUAN! IS IT TOO LATE TO PERFORM AT YOUR PARTY?
WOW. WHAT DID I SAY?
HONESTLY, IT'S FOR THE BEST.
HISS!
BARK!
RIBBIT!
TWEET!
END

WATCH OUT FOR PAPERCUTZ

Welcome to the explosively, eruptive, eleventh THE LOUD HOUSE graphic novel "Who's the Loudest?," from Papercutz, those chatterboxes dedicated to publishing great graphic novels for all ages. I'm Jim Salicrup, Editor-in-Chief and Honorary Member of the Low Talkers of America. After all the hubbub in this especially noisy volume of THE LOUD HOUSE (Guess they're not called Loud for nothing!) we thought it might be fun to figure out which was the loudest Papercutz graphic novel series. And yes, we know that technically all Papercutz graphic novels are silent, but we're judging by the amount of sound the word balloons and sound effects are indicating. And believe it or not THE LOUD HOUSE, by comparison, may not be that noisy after all. So, let's look at the runners up and reveal the noisiest Papercutz graphic novel series of all…

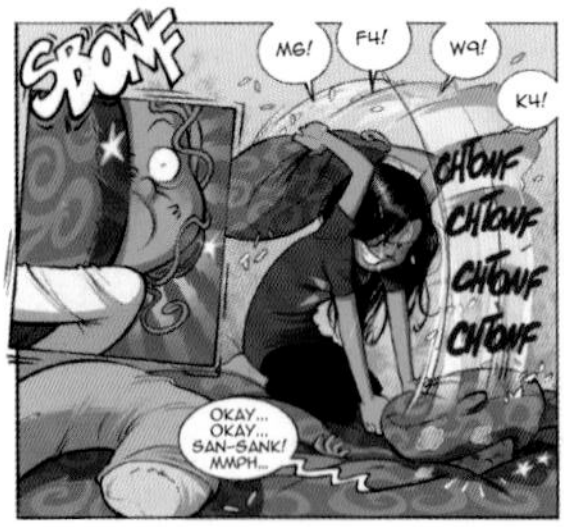
SBONF
MG!
FU!
WA!
KH!
CHTONF
CHTONF
CHTONF
CHTONF
OKAY... OKAY... SAN-SANK! MMPH...

THE SISTERS (by Cazenove and William) are Wendy and her younger sibling Maureen. Even though their house is inhabited just by the two of them and their parents, they can get awfully loud. Here they are playing a friendly game of Battleship. You should see and hear them when they're actually fighting with each other.

Things can get literally explosive in Papa Smurfs laboratory, when an experiment goes wrong, or when someone opens one of Jokey Smurf's presents. THE SMURFS TALES (by Peyo), can get raucous, especially when the Smurfs Village is invaded by Purple Smurfs…

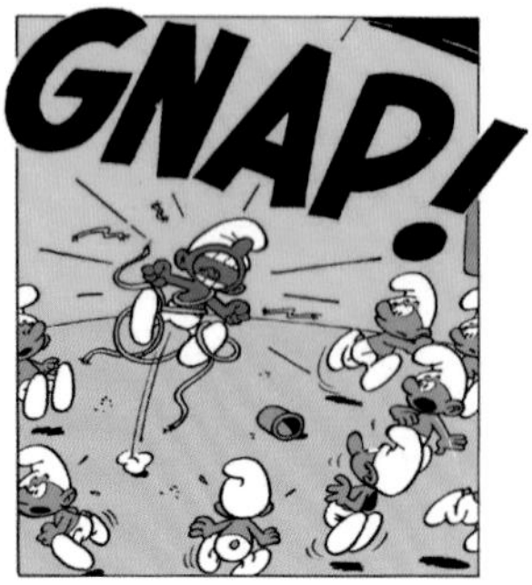
GNAP!

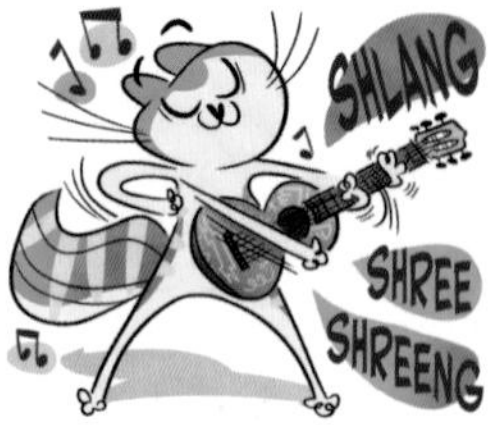
SHLANG
SHREE
SHREENG

In CAT & CAT (by Cazenove & Richez and Ramon), Catherine and her Cat, Sushi, and her dad, Nathan, are all far from being soft-spoken types. You wouldn't think one cat could cause so much calamity, but if you met Sushi, you'd know better. Sushi even has a noisy fantasy life…

Back in 50 BC, two warriors from a small village in Gaul, have been known to raise a ruckus while fending off the Roman Empire's legionaries. There's even a bard named Cacofonix and each book usually

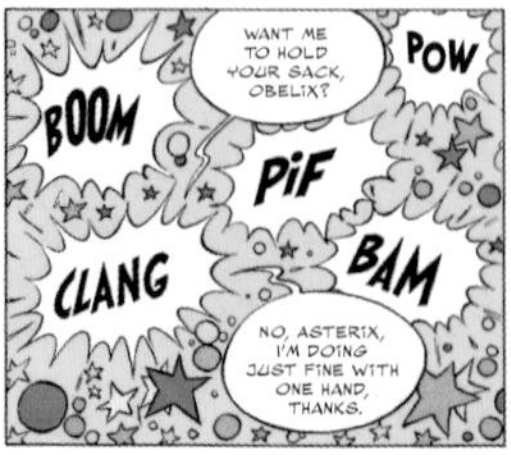
WANT ME TO HOLD YOUR SACK, OBELIX?
POW
BOOM
PiF
CLANG
BAM
NO, ASTERIX, I'M DOING JUST FINE WITH ONE HAND, THANKS.

ends with a raucous celebratory feast. Sometimes in ASTERIX (by René Goscinny and Albert Uderzo), Asterix and Obelix are overshadowed by the sounds of battle…

But we have to go back even further in time to find the noisiest Papercutz graphic novel series of all—DINOSAUR EXPLORERS (by Redcode, Albbie, and Air Team). While there are moments of quiet for Sean, Stone, Rain, Emily, Dr. Da Vinci, Diana, and Starz, the DINOSAUR EXPLORERS, once they're under attack by the prehistoric beasts there's a whole lot of shouting and screaming, not to mention roaring.

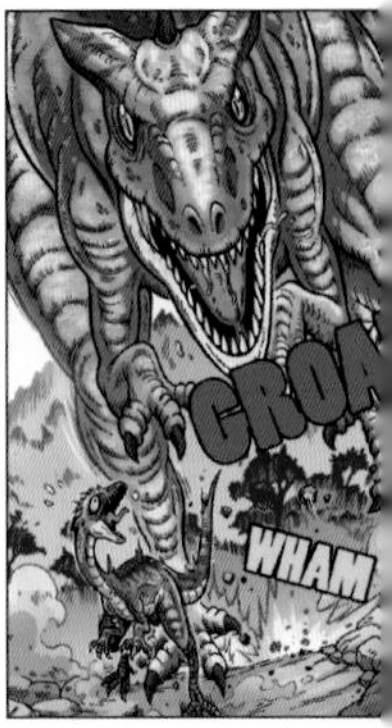
WHAM

After all that noise you may want to seek out a quiet place. Our favorite quiet place, aside from the palatial Papercutz offices when almost the entire staff is working at home, is our friendly neighborhood library. While during these crazy times we can't hang out there much anymore, we can still borrow books. Even Papercutz graphic novels, such as THE LOUD HOUSE #12 "The Case of the Stolen Drawers" are available at most libraries, not to mention booksellers everywhere. Just remember to be quiet at the library… you don't want to get shushed!

Thanks, Jim

STAY IN TOUCH!

EMAIL:	salicrup@papercutz.com
WEB:	papercutz.com
TWITTER:	@papercutzgn
INSTAGRAM:	@papercutzgn
FACEBOOK:	PAPERCUTZGRAPHICNOVELS
FANMAIL:	Papercutz, 160 Broadway, Suite 700, East Wing, New York, NY 10038

Chill out with a special preview of THE LOUD HOUSE Winter Special!

"OPERATION: X-MAS"

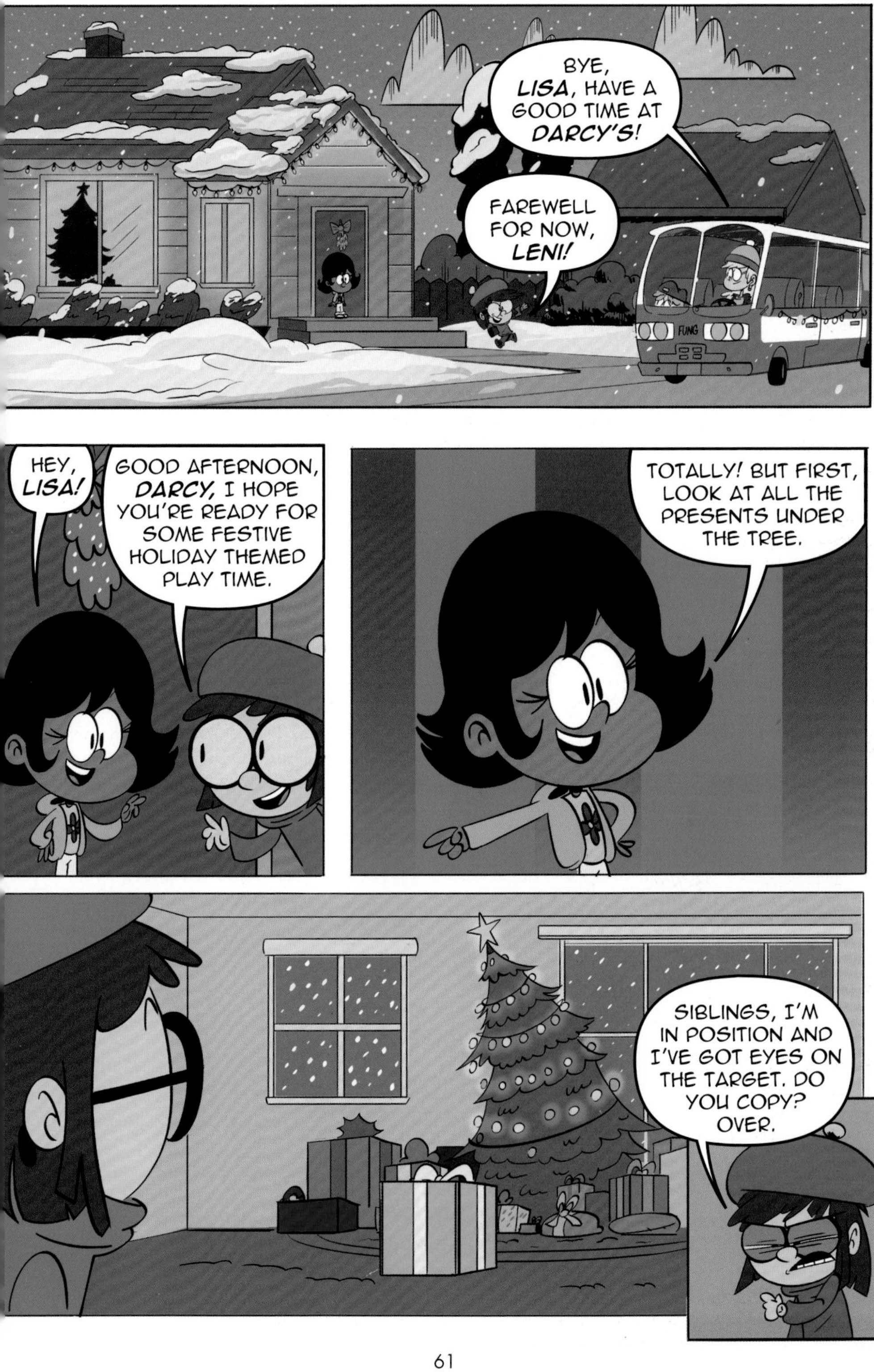
BYE, LISA, HAVE A GOOD TIME AT DARCY'S!
FAREWELL FOR NOW, LENI!
FUNG
HEY, LISA!
GOOD AFTERNOON, DARCY, I HOPE YOU'RE READY FOR SOME FESTIVE HOLIDAY THEMED PLAY TIME.
TOTALLY! BUT FIRST, LOOK AT ALL THE PRESENTS UNDER THE TREE.
SIBLINGS, I'M IN POSITION AND I'VE GOT EYES ON THE TARGET. DO YOU COPY? OVER.

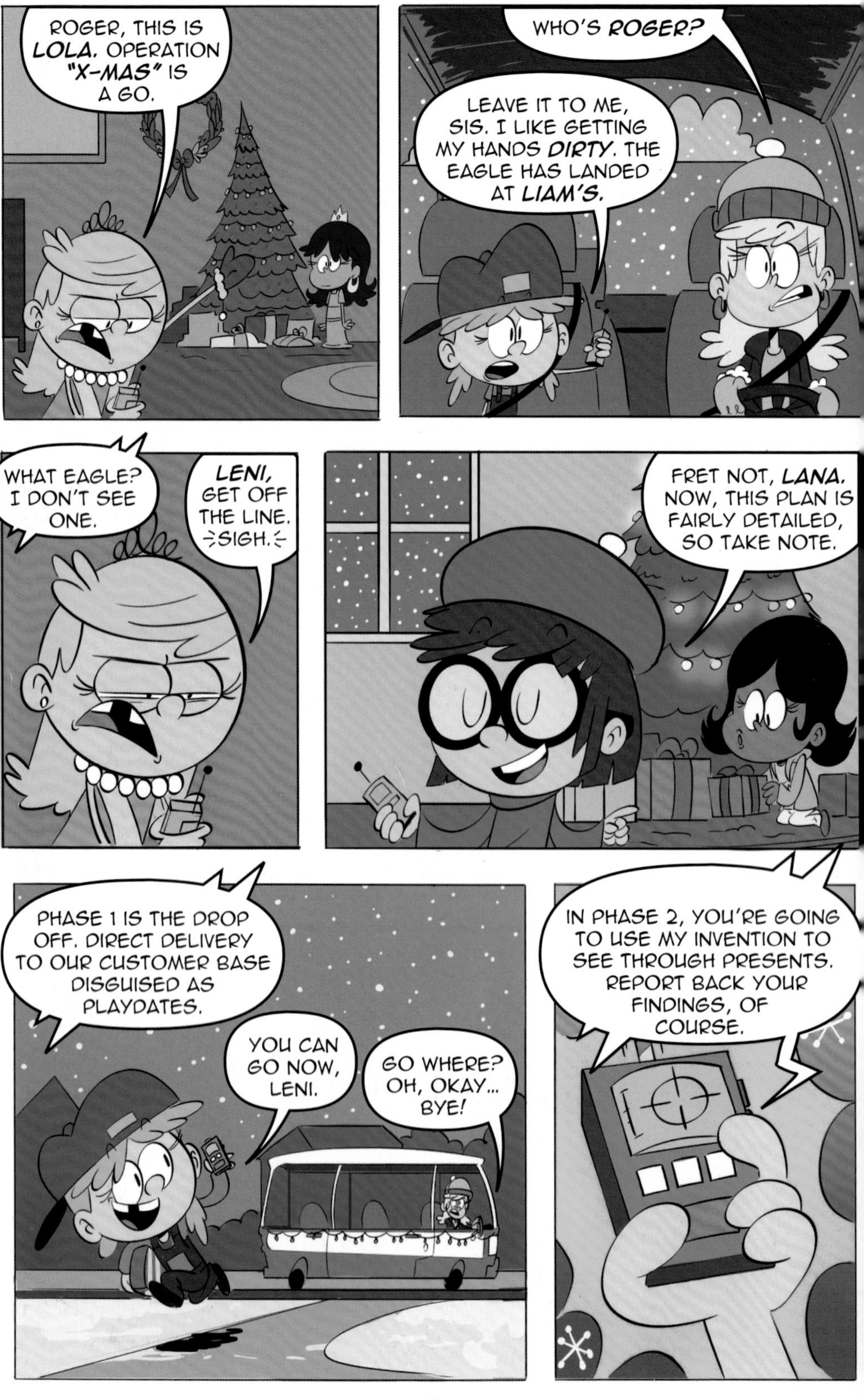
ROGER, THIS IS LOLA. OPERATION "X-MAS" IS A GO.
WHO'S ROGER?
LEAVE IT TO ME, SIS. I LIKE GETTING MY HANDS DIRTY. THE EAGLE HAS LANDED AT LIAM'S.
WHAT EAGLE? I DON'T SEE ONE.
LENI, GET OFF THE LINE. -SIGH.-
FRET NOT, LANA. NOW, THIS PLAN IS FAIRLY DETAILED, SO TAKE NOTE.
PHASE 1 IS THE DROP OFF. DIRECT DELIVERY TO OUR CUSTOMER BASE DISGUISED AS PLAYDATES.
YOU CAN GO NOW, LENI.
GO WHERE? OH, OKAY... BYE!
IN PHASE 2, YOU'RE GOING TO USE MY INVENTION TO SEE THROUGH PRESENTS. REPORT BACK YOUR FINDINGS, OF COURSE.

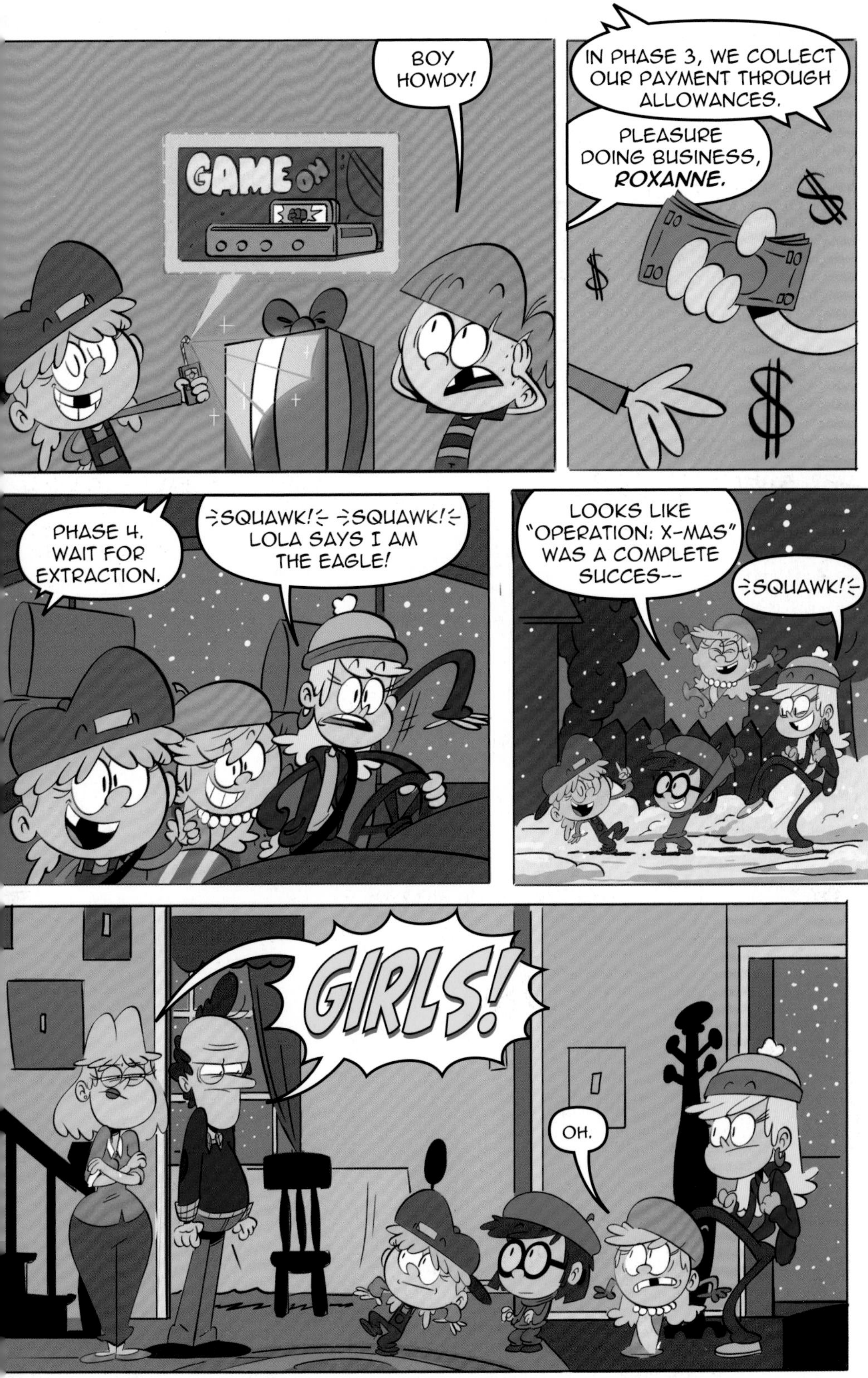
BOY HOWDY!
GAME ON
IN PHASE 3, WE COLLECT OUR PAYMENT THROUGH ALLOWANCES.
PLEASURE DOING BUSINESS, *ROXANNE.*
PHASE 4. WAIT FOR EXTRACTION.
SQUAWK! SQUAWK! LOLA SAYS I AM THE EAGLE!
LOOKS LIKE "OPERATION: X-MAS" WAS A COMPLETE SUCCES--
SQUAWK!
GIRLS!
OH.

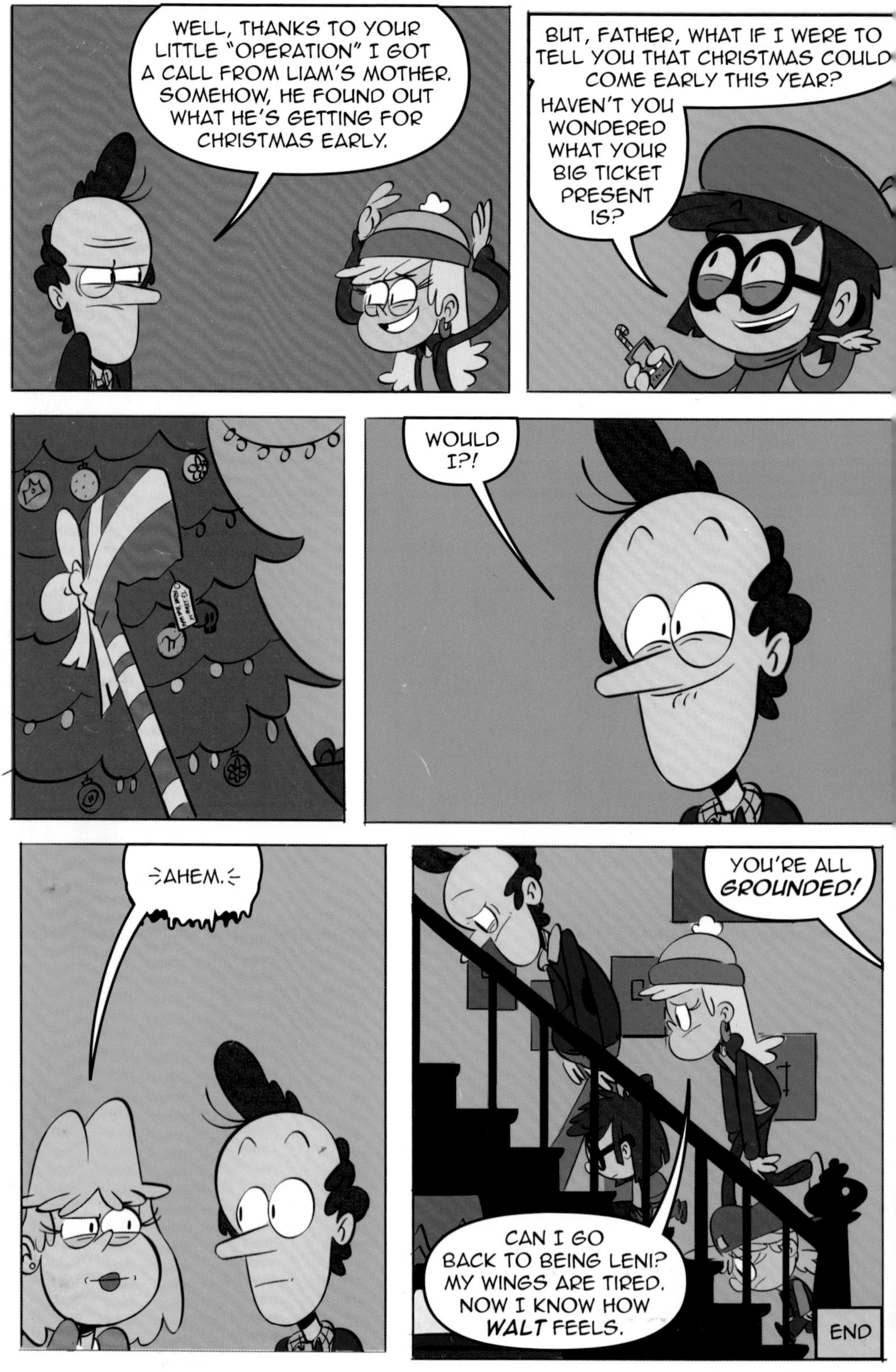
WELL, THANKS TO YOUR LITTLE "OPERATION" I GOT A CALL FROM LIAM'S MOTHER. SOMEHOW, HE FOUND OUT WHAT HE'S GETTING FOR CHRISTMAS EARLY.
BUT, FATHER, WHAT IF I WERE TO TELL YOU THAT CHRISTMAS COULD COME EARLY THIS YEAR?
HAVEN'T YOU WONDERED WHAT YOUR BIG TICKET PRESENT IS?
WOULD I?!
AHEM.
YOU'RE ALL *GROUNDED!*
CAN I GO BACK TO BEING LENI? MY WINGS ARE TIRED. NOW I KNOW HOW *WALT* FEELS.
END

THE LOUD HOUSE Winter Special is available now wherever books are sold.